Beneath the Lights

A NOVEL

BY

JIM BOYER

To my wife, who has been by my side encouraging me each step of the way.

"We can easily forgive a child who is afraid of the dark; the real tragedy of life is when men are afraid of the light."

— Plato

CONTENTS

ACKNOWLEDGMENTS

This book would not have been possible without the help and encouragement of my family and friends who read early drafts and provided both valuable feedback and constructive criticism. I also want to thank the guys from Thursday night book club for lowering your literary standards to read the nearly-final manuscript. I'm a better person for knowing each one of you.

PROLOGUE

Neil looked at his watch and took one last draw on his cigarette before tossing it on the ground and slipping through the opening in the fence. It was 11:10 PM, which meant Evelyn would already be on the amusement park grounds. His heart rate quickened as he made his way towards the Gold Nugget. If all went as planned, she would be dead within the hour.

CHAPTER 1

For some people the transition to adulthood is a subtle one that happens over time. They're shaped by the sum of their experiences, but the changes are almost imperceptible until much later in life. Others can look back and recognize a moment when that step into adulthood was a leap, and from that time forward they would never be the same. The summer of 1978 was that time for me. And although many years have passed since then, when I sit back and reflect on those months, every sound, every scent, and every emotion I experienced are as clear to me now as they were then.

I had just finished my freshman year studying Journalism at Franklin & Marshall College, a small but respected liberal arts school in Lancaster, Pennsylvania. I'm not completely sure how I had settled on Journalism as a major, but it was probably rooted in my views about the importance of truth. As a young boy growing up during the late 1960s and early 1970s, I enjoyed the same things as most kids. I spent my time playing baseball, avoiding homework, and terrorizing the neighborhood on my Schwinn Sting-Ray bike. It was a simpler time, and I have mostly good memories of it. But I was also oddly attracted to the current events unfolding at the time. While most other young people couldn't care less, I listened with curiosity as reports of the Watergate scandal, the Chappaquiddick incident, and the My Lai Massacre filled the evening news. What fascinated me the most was not so much that these things had occurred, but that each one came to light because someone wanted to know the truth and felt that others should know it too.

As I wrapped up my classes that first year of college, I was also getting ready to spend the first summer ever away from my family. My father worked at a U.S. manufacturing facility for a company based in West Germany. Several weeks earlier he had accepted a position at their corporate headquarters in Frankfurt, so my parents sold the house I had lived in all my life and packed everything into boxes. With bills to pay and my dorm closing for the summer, I needed to find a job that paid more than minimum wage and, just as important, a cheap place to live. I had almost given up when my roommate's father, who owned a construction company in a nearby town, offered me a job as a laborer and a room above their garage. He had landed several unexpected construction projects at a local amusement park and needed to hire some inexpensive temporary help. I fit the bill on both counts. To this day it's not clear whether he really needed my help or just took pity on me. Either way, I appreciated it immensely.

But more importantly, it was in June of that year that I met Evelyn. Well, I can't say I actually met her. She had died thirteen years before. But it was then that I first learned of her, and over the course of that summer my life became intertwined with her life, though hers had tragically ended more than a decade earlier.

May 26, 1978

The mid-morning sun streamed through the dorm window as I tossed my copy of *A Tale of Two Cities* onto the bed. It seemed odd to be saying goodbye to the place that had been my home for the past nine months, and I felt a trace of sadness as I looked over the empty shelves and the walls stripped of their posters. My belongings were mostly packed, and I figured I might have some time to start my assigned summer reading while I waited for the R.A. to check me out of the room. I looked around one last time to make sure I hadn't left anything in the drawers or under the bed, then settled onto the bare mattress with my book.

> *It was the best of times,*
> *it was the worst of times,*
> *it was the age of wisdom,*
> *it was the age of foolishness,*
> *it was the epoch of belief,*
> *it was the epoch of incredulity,*
> *it was the season of Light,*
> *it was the season of Darkness…*

That was as far as I got. My roommate, Jeff Hall, stuck his head into the room. He still hadn't started packing, and it seemed to be the furthest thing from his mind.

"Hey, Chad. Put that book down and come over to The Fack with me."

The Fack was short for the Fackenthal Library, a building I'm pretty sure he had never set foot in.

"What could possibly be going on in the library you'd be interested in?" I asked.

"Not IN the library, you moron. On the lawn. There's an ultimate frisbee game going on and Jessie Sanders is playing. She's wearing jean shorts and a bikini top that might not stay in place. I want to be there if anything happens."

"I should have known," I replied. "As tempting as that is, I need to wait here to check out."

"Are you kidding me? You've had your eye on Jess all semester. Maybe you'll even get up the nerve to ask her out afterwards."

"First of all, she doesn't even know who I am, and second, she'd probably never go out with me if she did. Besides, I need to get out of here and get to the airport to see Mom and Dad off."

"Ok, your loss buddy. I'll give you a complete description later," he said with a grin. "Tell your parents I said 'hi' and to have a safe flight."

"Will do. See you later tonight!" I shouted after Jeff as he hurried down the hallway.

Everyone liked Jeff. He was a handsome guy with a great sense of humor. His dirty-blonde hair always looked as if he had just gotten out of bed, but that never seemed to bother him…or any of the women he knew. Most people thought he was just plain goofy, but occasionally he would exhibit a stroke of genius that made you wonder whether he might just be much smarter than he acted. We were assigned to the same dorm room at the beginning of the school year and, while some of my classmates weren't very lucky when it came to the roommate lottery, I felt like I made out pretty well. In the short time we had known one another, Jeff had become one of my closest friends and someone I knew I could trust.

Thirty minutes later I was finally checked out and carrying the last of my things down to my orange '75 VW Scirocco. Until a few weeks earlier, the car belonged to my dad. But with no need for it while he was out of the county, he had passed it on to me. He loved that car, and I kidded him that he'd probably miss it more than he missed me. I was actually very grateful for it, since I could barely afford to buy any car of my own, let alone one that nice. The small hatchback was packed full, and I forced the lift gate closed. I drove through campus passing Manning Alumni Green and Old Main, a beautiful gothic revival building, before turning onto Harrisburg Avenue and heading out of Lancaster.

Traffic on the Pennsylvania Turnpike and Schuylkill Expressway was unusually light, and I arrived at the Philadelphia International Airport with plenty of time to spare. After dropping the car at short-term parking, I found my parents waiting at the Pan-Am gate in the international terminal. Mom looked a little down, but her face brightened as she saw me walking towards them.

"Chad, honey. I'm so glad you could make it to see us off."

"I wouldn't miss it for the world," I said. "Or for

Jessie Sanders," I added under my breath.

"Jessie who?" asked Mom. "Do you have a new girlfriend you're not telling us about?"

"Not likely," I said, and quickly changed the subject. "So, Dad, how are you holding up?"

"A little stressed, but I'm doing pretty well. This is a big change for us, and it's not easy leaving you here alone."

I rarely saw my father worried or upset. He worked tirelessly to provide for our family and, despite all the responsibilities that came along with his career, he took it all in stride and remained a steady force we could depend on. There had been times when his work took him away from our family for extended periods, and I knew it weighed heavily on him. He wasn't perfect and he would be the first to admit it, but he always taught me to do the best I possibly could and let the rest fall where it may. I owed much of who I was to him.

"I know you'll do great," I told him. "And don't worry about me at all. A little independence will be good for me. Haven't you always told me I needed to take more responsibility?"

"Yes, I know I've said that. But your Mom worries. Make sure you work really hard for Mr. Hall and try not to get into too much trouble while we're away."

"Don't worry Dad. How much trouble can a guy get

into living in central Pennsylvania? Nothing ever happens there," I joked.

We made some more small talk until it was time for them to board. Dad tried to slip me a twenty for gas before leaving, but I refused. It was a small gesture on his part to show he was concerned for me, and although I probably should have accepted it, I also felt the need to show him I would be fine on my own and that he didn't need to worry.

"Thanks, but you keep it," I said. "There's still some money left in my account, and I start my job in another week. I'll be fine."

He reluctantly put the bill back in his wallet, then looked up at me and said, "Oh, and whoever this Jessie person is you mentioned, she might be someone you should take a chance on. I'm not telling you what to do, but when I was your age, I almost didn't ask your mom out because I thought I didn't have a chance with her. That would have been the biggest mistake of my life."

"I know, Dad, but it's not that easy. She doesn't even know I exist."

"Well maybe it's time she did," he said as he reached out and squeezed my shoulder before turning to leave.

As I watched my parents walk through the gate towards their plane, I knew I'd miss them. But I also looked forward to the new possibilities that awaited being on my own for the summer. I stood in the terminal and watched through the large plate-glass windows until their Boeing 727 lifted off the runway, then headed back to Jeff's parent's place to unpack my things. As I made the trip back, I sensed there were bigger changes coming besides a new job and a different place to live. But I had yet to learn what they would be or how much they would impact me.

CHAPTER 2

<u>June 15, 1965</u>

Evelyn Welsh removed her sweater and threw it over her shoulder. The morning had warmed up considerably since she left her house on Cedar Avenue, and the walk to the amusement park was a pleasant one. The magnolia trees lining the road still held the last of their late spring blooms, and the scent hung lightly in the air.

She followed Ridge Road through the tunnel under the railroad tracks, crossed Park Boulevard, and entered the park through the south gate. Once inside, Evelyn took the small foot bridge over Spring Creek. As usual, she stopped on the bridge and dropped a leaf into the creek to watch the current carry it away. It was a ritual she performed almost every morning, but this particular time she watched the leaf much longer than usual, and found herself thinking how once it was set in motion it had no control over where it would end up or how it got there. When it was just a small speck downstream, she turned and continued on her way.

As she arrived at the main office of Hershey Park, she removed her employee identification card from her purse.

"Hi there, young lady," said Mr. Sensenig, the man responsible for managing the summer help. "You know you don't need to show me that every day. You've been working here for two weeks now."

Evelyn grinned sheepishly.

"I know. I can't help it. I just want to follow the rules."

"It's all right. I'm just giving you a hard time," he said with a smile. "Have you always been such a rule follower?"

She thought about it for a moment and answered, "Yes, I guess I have."

"Well, there's nothing wrong with that. In fact, there's not enough of that going around these days."

After checking her assignment for the day, Evelyn walked through the Kiddieland area of the park. She savored the warmth of the sun on her face as she passed the tiny Ferris Wheel and the Tubs-O-Fun on her way towards the Sky View. The Sky View was a two-person sky ride, and the boarding station was located at the top of a steep incline near the Midway. As its tiny ski-lift style chairs left the station, the ground sloped away and the riders were carried out over the crowd below. From this vantage point the passengers were treated to an aerial view of the Lost River boat ride and The Comet, the main roller coaster at Hershey Park. The Sky View continued over Spring Creek, made a turn, and came back to the station. It really wasn't much of a ride, but Evelyn enjoyed the view and liked talking to the passengers as she helped them into their seat and locked the safety bar across their laps.

As she walked up to the boarding station, she noticed a ladder leaning against one of the interior columns. A young man, who she recognized as one of the maintenance crew at the park, had the access door to the mechanical compartment open. His jeans and t-shirt were covered with grease and hydraulic fluid, and he was working methodically on the motor that drove the cable system. The morning heat had caused beads of sweat to form on his forehead, and they dripped onto the concrete floor below him as he worked. Evelyn looked up at him and smiled.

"Anything I can do to help?" she joked, brushing her hair behind her ear as she spoke.

"You're a little too late," answered the young man as he turned from his work and looked at her. "I'm just finishing up."

His hair was dark, almost black, and his brown eyes were deeply set. His frame was lean but muscular. He also had a slightly crooked nose that looked as if it had been broken at one time or another.

"You know, they just built this thing and it still needs to be hammered on at least once a week to keep it running," he said, descending the ladder. He wiped his greasy hands on his pants and extended his right hand towards her.

"I'm Neil."

"Evelyn."

"So, is this where they have you assigned today?" he asked, nodding his head towards the Sky View.

"You bet," she replied.

"Well if you have any problems with it, which wouldn't surprise me, just tell them to track me down. I'll be here all day."

"I'll do that," she said in a friendly tone and continued to watch him as he gathered up the last of his tools.

Evelyn was young, only sixteen, but seemed to have an innate ability to look right through someone and see things that others didn't. In fact, her friends often told her it was pointless to try to keep anything from her. As she looked him over, Neil fidgeted nervously.

"Well, it was good to meet you Evelyn," he said. "I'd stay and talk, but I'm needed over at the kiddie rides. Maybe I'll swing by later to make sure this is working okay."

"Thanks Neil," she said. "It was nice meeting you too."

She tilted her head and watched him curiously as he walked away. He had a rough look to him, and she knew right away he was the kind of guy her parents wouldn't like. He wasn't particularly handsome either, but there was something about him she found interesting. There was also something about him that made her uneasy.

June 5, 1978

I drove the Scirocco through the service entrance and pulled into an open parking spot. I had been to this amusement park many times before, but this would be the first time I wouldn't be entering through the main gate. As I climbed out of my car, I saw Jeff was already there leaning against a Hall Construction truck with a smile on his face and large cup of coffee in his hand. Several patches of his hair stood up at odd angles.

"You just get up?" I asked.

"Nope. Never went to bed."

"You're lucky your dad owns this company," I said, kicking off our normal exchange of friendly barbs.

"I can't argue with you there, buddy. Are you ready to get some blisters on those soft hands of yours?"

"Very funny. You act like I've never put in a hard day's work in my life."

"Well, have you?"

"Of course I have. But this will be the first time I've gotten paid more than three bucks an hour to do it."

"Yeah, Dad must have been really desperate for help."

I just shook my head and grinned. I was really looking forward to working with Jeff for the summer. His dad had done a huge favor for me, and as we walked through the side gate into the park I thought about how I didn't want to disappoint him.

The amusement park we'd be working at was Hershey Park, and was located in Hershey, Pennsylvania, home of the famous chocolate company. The park had been started in the early 1900s by Milton S. Hershey, founder of the Hershey Chocolate Company, as a place for his employees to relax and recreate during off hours. It was eventually opened to the public, and rides were added over the years as the popularity of the park continued to grow. Probably the most notable addition over that time was the first roller coaster, The Wildcat, constructed in 1923. This iconic coaster served the park for over twenty-two years until it was removed in September of 1945. Sadly, Milton Hershey passed away a month later.

The following year saw the introduction of The Comet, another classic wooden roller coaster added to take the place of the original Wildcat. By 1969 the park had grown in both size and popularity as the number of attractions increased, and a major redevelopment project was launched the following season. The extensive renovations continued for the next seven years and ended with the construction of the SooperDooperLooper, one of only a handful of looping roller coasters in the country at the time and the first on the East coast.

It was now 1978, and the park was continuing its efforts to update or remove old rides. On slate for demolition was the Gold Nugget shooting gallery, which would be our project for the next few weeks. The Gold Nugget originally began as a western-themed dark ride before it became a shooting gallery, and it had seen better days. Dark rides had been extremely popular in the late 1950s and 1960s, and were usually designed around a haunted house or fun house theme. The Gold Nugget was built in 1964 during the height of the dark ride era, and was the handiwork of Bill Tracy, the creative genius behind the Outdoor Dimensional Display Company. It featured two-person mine carts that carried riders past various mechanized special effects meant to scare, or at least surprise them.

By the mid to late 1970s, however, people were losing interest in this kind of entertainment and preferred the more exciting roller coasters and thrill rides. Vandalism had also taken its toll. The ride's dark corridors proved too inviting for young people looking to make trouble, and it was a regular occurrence for them to hop out of the carts, damage whatever they could, and return without being noticed. Even the chicken-wire screens added later to protect the fragile scenery did little to stop them. The owners of the park tried to extend the life of the attraction by converting it into a shooting gallery several years earlier, but now it was time to demolish the building to make room for the new Fender Bender bumper car ride. As I would soon find out, the Gold Nugget also had a dark and unsettling past the owners would be glad to put behind them.

CHAPTER 3

June 22, 1965

The week had gone by quickly for Evelyn. She was on a rotating schedule between several areas of the park, and enjoyed learning how to operate the different rides. She would often see Neil making his rounds, fixing anything and everything that needed attention. He was always quick to smile at her, and some of the uneasiness she had felt when they first met was beginning to fade away.

Neil didn't seem to get along as well with the management or the other employees, however. When he stopped by to talk to her, he often complained about his supervisor making life difficult for him. Neil was far more talented than any of the other maintenance crew there, but frequently wouldn't get the credit for his hard work. She learned he had ambitions to do much more with his life than fix rides at an amusement park, but as a high school dropout his options were limited.

Neil realized if he wanted to get anywhere in life he would have to make it happen himself. He told Evelyn he had been putting away every penny he could since he was twelve, and hoped to open his own repair shop. By the end of the summer, after seven years of saving, he would probably have enough to realize that dream. He had already accumulated most of the tools and equipment he would need, picking them up as cheaply as he could at auctions or going-out-of-business sales. An old family friend had even offered to lease him part of the warehouse building he owned, and the space would be available that September if he wanted it. After that, he joked, the only jerk he would ever have to work for again would be himself.

Their talks were pleasant enough, and she found herself looking forward to the times he would drop by. Today was one of those days, and she smiled to herself as she saw Neil approaching as she tended The Bug. A partially smoked cigarette hung from his mouth, and as he neared her he tossed it on the ground and stomped it out.

"You know you really shouldn't smoke those things," she said. "One of these days someone's going to figure out they're bad for you."

"I'm not worried kid," replied Neil. "It'll take a lot more than a few cigarettes to kill me. Besides, I don't think there's anyone around here who would care if something happened to me anyway."

"Don't say that. I'm sure there are plenty of people who would care."

"Well, I haven't met any of them yet," he said. "Except maybe you, from the way it sounds."

He winked as he said it, and Evelyn felt herself blushing. She glanced down so Neil wouldn't see that her cheeks had flushed, and as she did so she looked closely at his hands. His thumbs were hitched in the front pockets of his jeans, and she could see his hands were dirty and calloused. There were also several old scars on his knuckles, and she wondered if had gotten them from working or from fighting. She was immediately conscious of her own hands, smooth and nicely manicured, and how drastically different they were from Neil's.

Neil continued, "Say, I don't have a lot of time to talk right now, but I get off at five and was wondering if you wanted to do something after work."

"Oh Neil, I wish I could but I'm on until nine and then I work the early shift tomorrow morning."

He looked disappointed.

"That's alright, maybe some other time."

He began to walk away, then turned and said, "Or I could just come back when you're done. We could go on a few rides or something before you leave and you could still be home at a decent time."

Evelyn wasn't sure if it was a good idea. It didn't seem like Neil would take "no" for an answer, which worried her a bit. But she also found herself drawn to him in a strange and confusing way, and after giving it some more thought she agreed to spend the evening with him. Besides, it wasn't like it was an actual date or anything, and her parents would never have to know.

June 5, 1978

"Chad and Jeff, you'll be helping Hank with the demo work over at the Gold Nugget," ordered Mr. Hall.

Jeff and I nodded, grabbed our tool belts, and followed the foreman toward the center of the park. It would be several hours until it opened, but the place was already alive with activity as the staff made their preparations for the day. We walked past the Animal Gardens and then the Aquatheatre, where the dolphin and sea lion trainers were rehearsing for their shows that would take place later in the day. The Aquatheatre also hosted diving shows, where the performers would climb a narrow steel ladder to a platform far above the crowd before making the leap into the pool. I didn't mind heights to a certain point, but was pretty sure I would freeze if I ever had to make that climb. Fortunately, our work that day would be limited to the two-story wood frame building housing the Gold Nugget.

The plan was to gut the entire building, removing anything that could be reused or recycled, including the old mechanicals and background scenery. Once those were out, the entire building could be demolished. The vandalism that had occurred over the years had given us a head start, but we still worked carefully to preserve as much of the western-themed background and props as we could so they could be relocated to the Dry Gulch Railroad.

My job was to unbolt and remove any scrap metal, starting on the main level. Based on the amount of steel throughout the building, it seemed like it might take the entire summer just to accomplish that. Once I started, however, I moved efficiently through the corridors of the building removing any remnants of the old tracks and other items. By mid-morning I had worked my way through several rooms to the rear section of the building. Time passed quickly, and before I knew it Hank was sticking his head into the back room to let me know it was time to break for lunch.

"Let me just finish this section, then I'll stop," I yelled to Hank.

"Ok, but don't overdo it on your first day," he said. "I'm not sure why you would want to spend any extra time in here anyway. Especially in that room."

"What about this room?" I asked.

Hank stared at me with a puzzled look on his face.

"Do you mean you don't know?"

"Know what?"

"This is where she died."

I shuddered slightly as he said the words.

"Who died?"

As we sat in the shade eating our lunch, Hank told me the story of Evelyn Welsh and how her life had been stolen away one night in August of 1965. She was only sixteen at the time and was spending the summer as a seasonal employee at the park like so many other high school students had done over the years. Evelyn was a nice girl from a good family who had befriended Neil Fischer, a troubled young man who started working at Hershey Park after dropping out of high school. It was this friendship that cost Evelyn her life. One night she went to the park after closing and never returned. A horrific scene was discovered in the Gold Nugget where she had been brutally murdered, though her body was missing and had never been recovered. Neil Fischer was the main suspect due to his relationship with the girl, and was arrested the following week. He eventually confessed to the crime and was now serving a long prison sentence for third degree murder.

"The back room you were working in is where it happened," said Hank.

"Really?" I questioned in disbelief.

Why hadn't I heard about it before? I did some quick math in my head and figured I had only been five at the time, but I thought it would have at least come up at some point or another. My parents had never mentioned it on our many outings there over the years, but that wasn't necessarily surprising...it wasn't a subject I'd be quick to share with my child either. I also considered the possibility that Hank might just be pulling my leg since he had a reputation for messing with the new hires. But this time he wasn't. As I asked around later, I discovered every bit of it was true.

CHAPTER 4

June 22, 1965

About fifteen minutes before the end of her shift, Evelyn asked permission from Mr. Sensenig to clock out early and hurried to the ladies' room to check her hair and put on some lipstick. As she looked at herself in the mirror, she found herself wondering what is was that had made her feel so uneasy about Neil at first. Her thoughts were cut short, however, when she realized she only had a few minutes to get to the food stand where she and Neil had agreed to meet.

As she made her way through the park, the sun was dropping below the horizon. Lights blinked on at many of the rides and shops, and the illuminated neon tubes created a warm glow in the fading evening light. The aroma of popcorn and cotton candy drifted in the air, and

Evelyn breathed deeply as she took it all in. She thought about the warmth of the summer night, the anticipation of seeing Neil and the mixed feelings it gave her, and the joy of being young and having her whole life ahead of her.

Neil was already waiting when she arrived. He was wearing his usual plain white t-shirt and jeans, but they were clean this time. She could tell from his wet slicked-back hair he had also taken a shower.

"So, you made it," he said. "I thought you might have changed your mind."

"Not a chance. I wouldn't let you off that easy," answered Evelyn with a smile.

Neil pulled some change from his pocket and bought a bag of caramel corn, and they passed it back and forth as they strolled along the Midway, the main thoroughfare of the park. As they walked, she pointed out the rides she had operated so far that summer, and which were her favorites. He, in turn, described which ones he had worked on and which were the most difficult to repair.

"So how did you get so good at fixing things?" she asked.

"My dad taught me a lot of what I know, and the rest I figured out on my own," answered Neil. "It's the only halfway decent thing he ever did for me. In between giving me regular beatings for screwing up and sometimes putting his cigarettes out on me, he'd show me how to rebuild a carburetor or replace the piston rings on our old Ford."

"Well, at least he did that much for you."

"I guess so," he said, "But the funny thing is, he seemed to think it made up for all the bad stuff he did. It didn't though. That man had no business having a kid."

Suddenly, Evelyn felt very sad for him, and was beginning to see how Neil had been shaped into the person he had become.

"You know, Neil, I don't think anyone sets out to be a bad father. Some men just can't figure out how to be a good one."

"You've got that right," he said.

He appeared to be thinking about something, and then chuckled to himself.

"What is it?" asked Evelyn.

"I was just thinking about the time my old man taught me to fight."

"When was that?"

"I was in the first grade, believe it or not. One day on the playground this kid hit me over the head with a toy truck. It cut my head pretty badly, and I was still bleeding when I got home. When I told my dad what happened he wanted to know if I had done anything about it."

"Did you?" asked Evelyn.

"No, I just walked away. I mean, it didn't hurt that much and I knew the kid didn't try it, so it was no big deal."

"Well that's good."

Neil laughed.

"Dad didn't think so. He was so pissed he threw me in his pickup truck, drove me over to the kid's house, and told me we weren't leaving until I beat him up. So I did. It's not like I wanted to or anything, but afterwards I didn't even feel that bad about it."

In reality, not only did Neil not feel bad about it, he had actually enjoyed it. It was a welcome change being the one delivering the punishment rather than taking it, and for the first time in his young life he felt as if he was in control. After that he never backed down from another fight and, more often than not, he was the one looking to start one. But that wasn't something Neil could tell Evelyn. Not yet, anyway.

He continued, "I can still see the kid standing there with his nose bleeding and tears running down his face. He just looked at me like he couldn't understand what had just happened."

"Oh Neil, that's terrible! I can't believe your dad forced you to do that."

"I don't know…that's just the way he always was. Up until a few years ago, that is. He took off and we never saw him after that. Mom took it pretty hard at first. I'm not sure why, because he didn't treat her any better than he treated me."

"Does she still miss him?"

"Well, she died from a brain tumor last year, so I guess it's safe to say she doesn't."

"I'm so sorry about that. It must have been really difficult for you."

"Not really. I gave up on relying on anyone but myself long ago."

"Don't you think that's a little cynical?"

"No, I don't actually. It's just how it is. Anyway, I didn't ask you out so I could cry about my past. Let's forget about all that and try to have some fun."

As they walked they passed the Carousel and the Sky View and approached a building that looked like a series of old western store fronts. Large yellow letters reading "Gold Nugget" in a western style font stretched across the front of the building above the porch overhang, and a wooden Indian figure stood on the roof of the saloon at the far end. Strings of incandescent light bulbs hung between the poles marking the queue for waiting riders.

"Hey, let's go on this," suggested Neil, "It'll be fun."

Evelyn giggled and said, "I think you just want to get me in the dark, Neil Fischer."

But she agreed, and when they reached the front of the line they slid side-by-side into one of the mine carts queued up along the front of the building. The cart took off quickly and they were plunged into the darkness. The air smelled damp and musty. Neil and Evelyn could hear the clicking of the cart on the tracks as they entered the first corridor, and the screams and laughs of the other riders echoed through the building. A dim green bulb also lit the corridor, giving it an eerie glow.

As they approached the first turn they passed through a series of support beams resembling a mine shaft. A creaking sound could be heard, and the last beam appeared to crack and begin to fall onto the cart. It didn't, of course, and after the cart went by it returned to its place. They continued past other mechanized special effects, including a skeleton lighting a load of dynamite and an Indian jumping out from behind a rock. None of these were particularly alarming, but Evelyn did her part pretending to be scared. Halfway through the ride, Neil rested his arm on the seat behind her.

Evelyn, conscious of his arm against her back, paid less attention to what was going on around her. As they entered a bedroom with a sleeping woman, she certainly wasn't expecting her to sit up abruptly and scream. When she did, Evelyn jumped and pressed herself against Neil. She could smell the scent of his aftershave as she leaned in closer to him, and noticed how his clean white t-shirt glowed under the black lights used in the ride.

Their cart traveled down one last dark corridor before bursting through a set of swinging saloon doors, ending the ride. As they stopped behind the row of empty carts, Evelyn found herself wishing the ride was longer.

A light breeze blew as they walked towards the front gate at the end of the evening, and Evelyn pulled her sweater tighter around her shoulders. She hoped that Neil would take the cue that she was cold and put his arm around her again. But Neil did nothing more than walk closely by her side, allowing their arms to brush occasionally.

When they reached the gate, Neil turned to her.

"I had a nice time," he said. "Maybe we could do it again sometime. That is, if you want to."

"Sure, I mean, I didn't have an absolutely terrible time," joked Evelyn, trying not to sound too serious or too anxious.

Neil chuckled. "Ok, good. I'll see you around kid."

He nodded slightly at her as he often did and walked away.

June 7, 1978

After two days of back-breaking labor I had more than half the scrap metal removed from the Gold Nugget. It felt good to work hard and break a sweat. I tossed another load of rails and tie plates that had made up the cart tracks into a waiting dump truck, then stopped to rest for a moment. As I took off my hard hat and wiped my forehead, I looked up at the old frame building and found myself thinking about how many people had passed through it over the years. It seemed a shame to take it down but, given its history, it was probably for the best. My thoughts were interrupted by the Monorail humming by overhead, and I checked my watch. It was a little past 2:30, the time we usually stopped for our afternoon break. After checking in with Hank and letting him know I was going off the clock, I walked over to a nearby lemonade stand for a cold drink.

The story about Evelyn Welsh had raised my curiosity, and I wondered if any of the park staff who had been there at the time were still employed. The girl who took my drink order seemed friendly enough, so I decided to strike up a conversation.

"So, how long have you worked here?" I asked.

"This is my fourth summer," she replied. "But it will probably be my last. I'm transferring to another school on the west coast this fall, so I probably won't be around next summer."

"Do you know who's worked here the longest?"

"Oh, gee. I don't know. I think Mr. Sensenig has been here forever. He works in the main office scheduling the summer help."

"Is he there most of the time?"

"I think just in the morning. I always see him walking around the rest of the day checking on everyone. In fact, that's him over there by the kiddie coaster."

I looked towards where she was pointing, and saw a man of about fifty years of age talking to the ride attendant. He was short and stocky, and his hair was starting to go gray on the sides.

"Ok, thanks. I appreciate it. My name's Chad Anderson, by the way."

"I'm Cheryl," she replied, "Oh, and I met your friend Jeff the other day. He seemed really nice. I think he must have bought at least ten drinks from me since then."

I laughed to myself as I pictured Jeff putting the moves on her. Out of all his qualities, good or bad, I admired his confidence the most. Failure didn't seem to faze him at all, especially when it came to women. I wish I could have said the same for myself. Sure, I was comfortable around the opposite sex and had no real reason to doubt myself. As a young kid I was on the scrawny side, but by my sophomore year of high school my thin frame had filled out and I had become a reasonably good athlete. As a result, girls started to notice me. I had dated some since then and even had two brief relationships, one of which had ended badly. But certain women, like Jessie Sanders for example, left me at a complete loss. I could barely manage an awkward "hi" when I passed her on campus, and had convinced myself I was destined to admire her from a distance and nothing more.

Another customer came up behind me, so I thanked Cheryl again and headed back to find Hank. As I finished my lemonade and went back to work, I decided I would talk to Mr. Sensenig the first chance I could.

CHAPTER 5

July 12, 1965

For the past three weeks Neil and Evelyn had been nearly inseparable. She kept the relationship hidden from her parents for as long as she could, but eventually grew tired of making up stories about who she was with and where she was going. Her parents weren't happy about it, to say the least, but they learned a long time ago that once Evelyn made up her mind there was little they could do to change it. Even when she was only seven, she had insisted on wearing the same dress to school every day for two weeks. She didn't cry or throw a fit when they told her to change her clothes; she simply stared at them with a determination that told them to pick their battles carefully, because this was one they wouldn't win. After several days of facing off, her parents finally relented. It was only later they discovered a new student named Sarah had transferred to Evelyn's school, and her family could only afford one dress for their daughter. The girl had been ridiculed by her classmates, and this was Evelyn's solution to the problem. When it eventually occurred to her that she could give Sarah several of her own outfits, the two became fast friends and Evelyn returned to dressing normally.

At first her parents thought her relationship with Neil might be a repeat performance of that episode from years earlier. Evelyn was drawn to the most unlikely of people. But they had always hoped she would date someone from a solid local family, preferably the son of one of their country club friends, and if not that, at least someone with college and a promising career in his future. They certainly hadn't pictured Evelyn getting involved with a high school drop-out with a history of rebelling against authority. Even his plans to start his own business hadn't impressed them. Evelyn assured them over and over that Neil was a decent guy despite his reputation to the contrary, but they still couldn't help feeling she was being naïve. They also felt her judgement was probably clouded by the fact that someone three years older was showing a genuine interest in her.

Now Evelyn stood with him outside his apartment. It was late, and Neil leaned against the side of his car, illuminated by the mercury-vapor lamp along the street. A wisp of smoke hung in the air above them and several cigarette butts littered the macadam at his feet. Evelyn faced him with her arms crossed in front of her. After a long silence, she was the first to speak.

"I don't know Neil. I don't think I can do this…I'm just not ready."

"Not ready? Are you kidding me?" He reached for her but she pulled away.

"I know your mind is made up, but I still need some time to think."

"The time for thinking is over. We've been over this so many times."

"I know how you feel, and I really care about you too. But we haven't been seeing each other very long. How can I be sure you won't change your mind about me?"

"I've never been more positive about anything. We just need to do it."

"Please stop putting so much pressure on me."

Out of frustration Neil reached out and grabbed her tightly by the arms. Evelyn winced in pain and pulled back again, this time slapping him across his right cheek.

"Don't ever touch me like that Neil!"

She buried her face in her hands and began to cry.

"Listen, I'm sorry," said Neil, "I shouldn't have done

that. I guess I just have too much of my father in me. I hate it, but I do. "

"It doesn't have to be that way."

"How could you possibly know that? You haven't dealt with the things I've had to deal with, and you've been given advantages I'll never have. Did your Dad ever tell you he wished you'd never been born? Have you ever had to stand between your parents and take a beating so, just once, your Mom could get a break?

Evelyn didn't answer.

"I didn't think so," he said.

"You're not your father," she said wiping her eyes on her sleeve.

"Maybe not. But I'm still a Fischer and I carry the weight of that name. I'm not sure I can get out from under it."

"I think you can."

"We'll see about that," he answered. "Now get in the car. I'm taking you home."

June 15, 1978

More than a week after my conversation with Cheryl, I finally had an opportunity to talk to Mr. Sensenig. As I finished up for the day and packed away my tools, he walked by the fenced-off work area near the Gold Nugget. It seemed like as good a time as any, so I flagged him down and asked to speak with him.

"I'm really sorry to bother you, but I was wondering if you had a few minutes," I asked.

He looked annoyed.

"What do you want?"

"I understand you've worked here quite a while."

"Yes," he said impatiently. "More than twenty years. Why do you ask?"

"I was wondering if you could tell me anything about Evelyn Welsh's death."

His face softened a bit at the mention of her name.

"Why are you asking? You're certainly too young to have known her."

"No, I'm just curious. I had never heard about her until I started working here recently."

"Well, there's not much to tell. She was a lovely young girl that made some bad decisions."

"Bad decisions?" I asked.

"Getting involved with the wrong person, for one. That was her biggest mistake," he answered, referring to Neil.

"Were there more?"

He hesitated. "Nothing other than rumors. Some

51

people thought she wasn't as innocent as she appeared, but I didn't believe any of it and I really don't want to elaborate. What's done is done, and it won't help her at all now to dredge up a bunch of hearsay that may not even be true."

"What about Neil Fischer? What was he like?"

"Well, he had a temper, that's for sure. And he didn't like being told what to do."

Mr. Sensenig continued, "I remember soon after he started working here, in 1964 or so, he had a run-in with one of the maintenance supervisors. Joe Peterson was his name. Now this guy was no saint himself, and would always give Neil a hard time. One time he laid into Neil for damaging some piece of equipment or the other, but it was really Joe that had done it. Neil wasn't going to stand for it, and an argument started, which turned into a fight. Neil beat him so badly he ended up in the hospital."

"But why didn't he get fired? Or arrested?"

"In the end Joe admitted it was all his fault. He didn't press charges for the beating he took, and the management decided to give them both another chance. Joe never tried to cross Neil again though. In fact, it seemed like they may have even respected each other after that. Neil for dishing out the beating, and Joe for not pressing charges afterwards."

"So, they became friends?"

"No, I didn't say that. Neil wasn't interested in making friends. He didn't see the need for them."

"But he was friends with Evelyn, right?"

"Yes, but that was different. She was a beautiful girl and Neil was attracted to her, and I don't think his intentions were honorable. I'm sure you know what I mean by that."

"Yes sir, I do."

I thanked Mr. Sensenig for taking the time to talk to me. As he started to walk away, he turned and looked at me again.

"One more thing I can tell you is that I'm glad to see that place go." He nodded his head in the direction of the Gold Nugget. "That thing should have been torn down years ago."

CHAPTER 6

August 24, 1965

Detective Vaughn waited patiently for the forensics unit to arrive. He had arrived at the park an hour earlier, met by Richard Barr, an older man who was head of park security. Earlier that night, John and Doris Welsh became concerned when their daughter failed to return home after what should have been a quick trip to the park. According to her parents, she had left her purse there earlier in the day. Evelyn left the house around 10:45 PM and was only planning to be gone long enough to retrieve it, but after several hours she hadn't returned and they began to worry.

It was now 3:00 in the morning. Mr. Barr, who was on duty that night, had seen Evelyn arrive and talked to her briefly. After being informed that she never made it home, he had scoured most of the park looking for her before coming upon the grisly scene in a back room of the Gold Nugget. A large pool of blood covered the floor. Two trails of smeared blood stretched from the pool to the nearest exit where someone had apparently been dragged towards the door. Several boot prints were also visible. Based on the detective's observations, there were no other signs of a struggle. Death must have come quickly, he thought.

"Is everything as you found it?" the detective asked.

"Yes sir. I called for the police right away," answered Mr. Barr.

"And you're sure you didn't touch anything?"

"Positive."

"Okay, we need to make sure nobody gets in this building before my forensics person gets here."

Mr. Barr nodded. His face was pale and he didn't look well.

"Are you okay?" asked Detective Vaughn.

"Not really. I'm used to the occasional petty theft at one of our shops or dealing with one of our customers when they get a little rowdy, but not this kind of thing. I've worked here for thirty years and I've never seen anything like this. There's so much blood."

The detective nodded in understanding. It didn't matter how many times he had seen this. It was never easy and he had never gotten used to it.

"You know, I was planning to retire at the end of this season," said Mr. Barr. "This isn't the way I wanted to end things here."

"How do you mean?" asked the detective.

"Evelyn was such a sweet girl. I knew I should have insisted on staying with her while she got her purse. I feel like this could have been avoided."

"I know it seems certain what you found here is related to Evelyn, but it might not be. In fact, we have other officers out looking for her right now. We just don't know for sure that this has anything to do with her…unless there's something you're not telling me."

"No, just a bad feeling. It's the same feeling I'd always get when I'd see her and Neil together."

"I see," said Detective Vaughn.

As he looked over the room, he added, "By the way, did Evelyn happen to say where she had left her purse? It might be helpful to retrace where in the park she might have been tonight."

"No, I don't think she ever said."

"And you don't recall seeing it anywhere when you were searching for her?"

"No sir, I don't. But finding Evelyn, not her purse, was my main concern."

"I understand," said the detective as the forensics team finally arrived at the Gold Nugget. "Thanks for your help, Mr. Barr. I'll be in contact with you if I have any further questions. Now if you'll excuse me, we have a lot of work to do here before the park opens."

June 20, 1978

Another long work day was finally over, and Jeff and I relaxed in his room. I was sprawled out on the bean bag chair in the corner while Jeff, who had just taken a shower, picked out a shirt from his closet. It was still early in the summer and the projects at Hershey Park were progressing well, so Mr. Hall had generously decided to purchase evening tickets to the park for any of his employees that wanted them. I decided to take advantage of the offer, and asked Jeff if he was planning to do the same.

"Sorry Chad. I can't tonight. I have a big date with that girl from the lemonade stand."

"You mean Cheryl?"

"Uh, yeah, I think that might be her name," he answered as he buttoned up the wide-collared silk shirt he had chosen.

I just shook my head. Jeff never failed to amaze me.

"You know she's moving away at the end of the

summer, right?" I asked.

"Of course I do. Isn't it great?"

"It is?"

"Sure, I can't think of a better situation," replied Jeff with a big grin.

He grabbed his bottle of Hai Karate aftershave and splashed a large handful onto his neck and face, then looked at me self-consciously.

"Do you think that's a little too much?"

"Not at all. It goes with the rest of your approach."

I left him to plan his treachery and headed back to my room to clean up and put on a change of clothes. It was around 7:00 that evening when I returned to the park and presented my ticket at the main gate. It would have been more fun with Jeff along...almost everything was, but I decided to make the most of it.

I hadn't eaten anything since my lunch break, so I grabbed a hot dog and soda at the food court in the center of the park. I ate as I walked, taking in the sights. It had been a busy day there, and I watched the parents as they dragged their kids from ride to ride. After a full day at the park, most of them were starting to melt down. Nearby, a little girl screamed because her ice cream cone had chocolate sprinkles instead of rainbow sprinkles. I made a mental note to avoid having children until I was at least thirty, and strolled past the Himalaya towards the SooperDooperLooper. The looping coaster was Hershey Park's most popular ride since it had opened the year before, but the lines were surprisingly short, so I rode it several times before deciding to try my hand at a few games.

I approached the Whack-a-Mole game, where two young boys were waiting for a third person to show up so they could play. This should be easy, I thought as I plopped down my quarters and grabbed the padded mallet. The red-headed kid to my left got off to a quick start but, as expected, I made a strong comeback and collected a small stuffed giraffe as the spoils of my victory. I didn't really want it and was about to hand it to the red-headed kid, but changed my mind when he gave me dirty look and made a suggestion about where I could put it.

"Keep practicing kid," I said and walked away with the giraffe.

By that time the evening twilight had faded, and the incandescent tracer lights running along the hand rails of The Comet had been turned on. I had always felt that after dark was the best time to ride the old wooden coaster, so I stepped into the queue and waited on the ramp for the line to move forward. When it finally reached the top and my turn came, I slipped into an open car at the front. I was about to lower the safety bar when I heard a voice at my side.

"Is this seat taken?

I looked up to see who had spoken. It was Jessie Sanders.

My heart started to race and my palms began to sweat.

"Uh, sure. I mean, no, it's not taken," I said, stumbling over my words.

"Thanks!" she said cheerfully and slid into the spot next to me. "My friends are a few cars back. There's three of us, so we had to split up."

I waited for her to buckle her lap belt, and then carefully pulled down the safety bar. As I looked down I saw the stuffed animal by my side and, feeling self-conscious about it, tried to push it down at my feet where she wouldn't be able to see it. It was too late.

"Nice giraffe," said Jess, "Do you always bring him with you?"

I mentally kicked myself for not giving it to the red-headed kid earlier, but then decided to make light of it.

"Yes, as a matter of fact, I do. I guess you caught me."

Before she could say anything more, the line of bright red cars jerked into motion and began the slow climb up the first hill. The gears clicked and rattled as the cars gained elevation.

"You're Chad, right?" asked Jess. "Don't you go to Franklin and Marshall?"

I was surprised she recognized me, and even more shocked she knew my name.

"Yeah, and you're, uh, Jessie Sanders, right?" I answered, trying to pretend I needed to search my memory for her name, when in reality, I thought about her several times a day.

"Yes, but most people just call me Jess. You can too if you want."

We reached the top, and the car descended quickly down the first and largest of the drops. I had never felt my stomach leap so far up into my chest before on The Comet, but I had also never ridden it with Jessie Sanders. The lights on the railings rushed by, and as we flew around each curve the force slid us against each other. I could feel the warmth of her shoulder and hip pressing against mine, and decided it was definitely more fun without Jeff along.

The coaster made the last turn and came to an abrupt halt in the station. As we waited for the safety bar to unlock, Jess explained that she was living back home in Maryland for the summer and had come up for the day with her friends.

"Thanks for letting me share the ride," she said, "I guess I'll see you on campus when school starts up again."

"I'm looking forward to it," I answered. "And here, I want you to have this."

I handed her the giraffe.

"Aw, thanks!" she said with a smile. "But won't you miss it?"

"To be honest, we really weren't that attached."

"Well, okay. In that case, I'll keep it on my bed and think of you whenever I look at it."

I could feel my palms start to sweat again.

"There is one condition though," I told her, knowing if I didn't take a risk I would hate myself afterwards. "I'm going to need your phone number so I can check up on him."

She laughed and said, "Wow, that's pretty smooth, Chad."

I had to laugh too because I'd never been called smooth by anyone, especially not by someone like Jessie Sanders. To my surprise, she borrowed a pen and scrap of paper from a nearby ice cream vendor, wrote down her number, and slipped it into my hand. I watched her walk back to her friends waiting on the concourse just outside the coaster. She showed them the stuffed animal, and as they all looked over at me and whispered to each other, I felt my face turn a bright red. Fortunately, I was too far away for them to notice. And as Jess turned back and waved to me, my embarrassment was replaced with a smile that formed slowly and remained long after I left the park that evening.

CHAPTER 7

<u>August 25, 1965</u>

"Thanks for the coffee, Mrs. Welsh. You really shouldn't have gone to the trouble," said Detective Vaughn.

"Oh, I don't mind at all. I worry less if I'm busy," she answered, straightening the magazines on the cocktail table for the third time.

"Well, I appreciate it. Is there anything else at all you can tell me that might be helpful?"

The Welsh's had already recounted how Evelyn had started working at Hershey Park at the beginning of the summer, and how she had always been a good girl that had never been in any kind of trouble. They had begun to have concerns that she was spending so much time with Neil Fischer, however. He seemed like bad news, and they didn't know what their daughter could possibly see in him.

He was a high school drop out without much of a future. There were also the bruises. Several times over the last two months they had noticed bruises on their daughter's body. Evelyn usually laughed it off and made an excuse that she had clumsily bumped into something at work or had slipped and fallen. Doris told the detective that she had suspicions all along that the bruises had come from Neil, but had hesitated to say anything since Evelyn seemed happy and described him as a good friend. Now she was regretting her decision to brush it off. Her daughter was missing and it seemed certain something terrible had happened to her.

"I feel so helpless. I can't bear to think about Evelyn suffering," she said and began to sob.

"Listen, Mrs. Welsh," said Detective Vaughn, trying to comfort her. "We don't know for certain that what we found at the park had anything to do with Evelyn. We have a lot of people out looking for her."

"Did anyone at the park see her at all?" asked John Welsh.

"Richard Barr, the head of security, saw her arrive there some time after 11:00 PM. He said he offered to walk along with her while she got her purse, but she told him she was fine and not to bother. He didn't run into her again after that, so he assumed she had left and he just hadn't seen her. He was very broken up about it and regrets not staying with here."

"Was anyone else there?"

"The place was pretty empty last night. Two maintenance workers were the only other employees around, and they were tied up doing repairs at the far end of the property."

"Was one of them Neil Fischer?"

"No. Neil wasn't scheduled to work that evening, but it's possible he could have been somewhere on the grounds. He hasn't been at his apartment at all, but we have a squad car waiting there for him in case he shows up."

"Do you think he was responsible for this?" questioned Mrs. Welsh.

"We don't know. But he's definitely a person of interest. We're also questioning her friends and co-workers to see if we can get any other leads."

"Ok," she said as she dried her eyes, "Please tell us what you find out. And let us know if we can do anything more to help."

"I'll do that," assured the detective as he shook John Welsh's hand and pulled the door open to leave.

June 24, 1978

The town's public library was housed in the Hershey Community Center, a stately five-story Indiana limestone building between Chocolate Avenue and East Caracas Avenue. I pulled into the parking lot soon after it opened. It wasn't how I would normally spend a Saturday morning, but the story of Evelyn's death had really gotten to me and I wanted to find out as much as I could. The conversation with Mr. Sensenig had only piqued my interest more.

The librarian helped me find the microfiche of the local newspapers from the week of the murder, the day Neil Fischer was arrested, and from months later when he was sentenced. I settled in at the microfiche reader and remained there for several hours.

As I scanned through the articles and pictures, I saw Evelyn for the first time. On August 25th the newspaper had run her freshman yearbook photo, and it appeared many times throughout archived articles. I'm not sure what I expected her to look like, but she had an innocent beauty that was disarming. Her hair was a very light blonde, and she wore it in a short shoulder-length bob, parted in the middle and curled slightly inward at the bottom. The article described her as having blue eyes and, although the picture was printed in black and white, they drew me in in a way I couldn't have explained if I tried. She also wore a wry smile that seemed to indicate she wasn't comfortable having her picture taken, and I felt sad for her.

Looking at her picture, I thought about the rumors Mr. Sensenig had mentioned during our conversation. Somehow it felt wrong to think that she wasn't the sweet young girl she appeared to be, but I knew that was probably naïve on my part. She wouldn't have been the first teenager to hide things from her parents, especially if they had such high expectations for her.

In the days following Evelyn's disappearance, search teams made up of local police and volunteers scoured the area around Hershey. The Pennsylvania State Police were called in to assist shortly afterwards as no leads were found and the search area grew larger. One article included a picture of John and Doris Welsh being interviewed on their front porch, and the strain showed on their faces as they talked about their daughter and begged anyone with knowledge of her whereabouts to come forward. John was a successful businessman and Doris was a former beauty queen and actress, now very much involved in society events around Hershey. But it was clear that either one of them would have gladly given up everything they had to get their daughter back.

Blood typing had been completed on samples recovered from the crime scene and confirmed that it was a match to Evelyn's blood type. While this certainly didn't prove it was hers, the fact that less than 10% of the population was O-negative indicated that it very likely was.

According to the articles, Neil Fischer had been a suspect in Evelyn's disappearance almost immediately. These suspicions were further confirmed when Neil didn't return to his apartment or show up for work the following day. Also, bloody shoe prints found at the scene matched the type of work boots he was known to wear. Finding out more information about Neil or where he might have gone proved difficult, since he had little family in the area and few friends.

The first of two major breaks in the case came on August 28th. A search team covering a stretch of public land outside Hershey found a bill of sale for some auto parts Neil had purchased. This led them to focus their efforts on a wooded area nearby, where they discovered a partially buried plastic bag. The bag contained a pair of shoes and several articles of clothing matching those Evelyn wore the night she disappeared. The items were positively identified as hers, and the chances of finding the girl alive seemed even more remote than before.

The second break came on August 31st. News of the

apparent murder and the ensuing manhunt had spread through the mid-Atlantic region, and a waitress in a diner in upstate New York recognized a man matching Neil's description. An off-duty police officer happened to be in the diner at the time and detained him until backup could arrive. Word traveled fast that Neil Fischer had been arrested. Within days he confessed to the murder of Evelyn Welsh.

CHAPTER 8

August 27, 1965

Detective Vaughn pulled up in front of Sarah Witmer's home and turned off the engine. As he made his way up the front walk he could see the house was dark. A knock on the front door confirmed that no one was home, so he returned to his car and waited. Large elm trees lined either side of the street, and the roadway glistened from the recent rain. As he waited, he flipped back through his notes. About twenty minutes later Sarah's car came slowly up the street and parked behind him. As she locked the car and walked across the lawn toward the house, the detective slid out of his car and called to her.

"Sarah Witmer?"

"Yes?" she replied suspiciously.

"I'm Detective Charles Vaughn," he said, showing her

his badge. "I'm investigating Evelyn Welsh's disappearance, and I was wondering if you might have time to answer a few questions for me."

"Oh my gosh, of course. Come in and we can talk."

Sarah unlocked the front door, switched on the light, and led Detective Vaughn into the living room.

"I just finished my shift at the diner. I work as many hours as I can get, so it's lucky you caught me."

The detective took a seat on the couch as Sarah set her purse and apron down on an end table.

"I'd offer you something to eat or drink, but my parents aren't around very much so I don't think there's anything here…unless you want a beer."

"No thanks," he replied with a smile. "Not while I'm working anyway. I really just want to know what you can tell me about Evelyn. I understand the two of you are close friends, so I thought you might be able to shed some light on things. You know, maybe give me some insight that I wouldn't be able to get from her parents."

"I'm not sure what I can tell you that would help. I heard Neil is a suspect and no one's been able to find him."

"That's correct. Do you think he was involved?"

"I guess it sure looks that way to everyone. But Evelyn never had anything bad to say about him. She thought he was just misunderstood and was really a decent guy. She also talked about how smart he was, and how he could fix anything."

"Did they spend a lot of time together?"

"Sure, especially the last few weeks. I think he really had a thing for her."

"Did they ever fight? Did he ever hurt her in anyway?" asked Detective Vaughn.

"Not that she ever said. But I did see them outside his apartment one time when I was driving home from the diner. It looked like they were arguing. She looked really irritated, and he looked like he was trying to convince her of something, or maybe talk her into doing something. I can't say much more than that because I was only driving by and didn't stop."

Charles thought about this and made a few scribbles in his notebook.

"Can you remember when that was?" he asked.

"I'm not sure. It was at least a month ago, maybe more."

After a few more routine questions which Sarah gladly answered, he thanked her and got up to leave. As he headed toward the front door, Sarah stammered slightly and then was quiet.

"Was there something else you wanted to tell me?"

"I don't know." She hesitated. "It's probably nothing."

"Maybe so. But I'd still like to hear it."

"I feel terrible even mentioning this, because it doesn't seem like Evelyn at all. She was always a better person than me, but she never made me feel like I wasn't good enough to be her friend."

"What is it?"

"I think she may have been doing drugs. Maybe heroin or something like that."

"Heroin?" asked the detective.

"Yeah, heroin. Like in the Velvet Underground song. You've heard of it, right?"

"Um, yes, I'm familiar with it. But how do you know enough about heroin to think Evelyn may have been doing it?"

"Like I said, I'm not a particularly good person."

Detective Vaughn nodded his head. "Go on."

"Anyway," continued Sarah, "she seemed depressed lately, like maybe things weren't going well at home. She was always tired too, and had bruises on her arms. At least I thought they were only bruises at first, but one day we were laying out in my backyard getting some sun and I got a closer look at them. They looked more like track marks."

"Did you ask her about them?"

"Of course I did, but she denied it and said I was

74

being ridiculous."

"It seems out of character for her though, doesn't it? Everyone I've talked to so far has said what a nice young woman she is and that she's never been in any kind of trouble."

"I know. It doesn't make sense. But nothing about this makes any sense."

Charles thought about the implications if Evelyn had been drawn into drug use, especially heroin. Its use had been well-documented in the music of recent years, contributing to its growing popularity among young people throughout the country. He was even seeing the drug surface more frequently in the local area, and the effects were sobering. Charles never had children of his own, but could sympathize with the parents of those who had fallen into its trap. For teenagers, every choice came with consequences, and as time passed the stakes became much higher. Sometimes those choices could be irreparable. He also knew he would need to detach himself from any emotions about the subject if he was going to do what was required of him.

June 24, 1978

After leaving the library I drove back to the Hall's and climbed the steps to my room above the garage. My eyes were tired from scanning the microfiche and a headache was forming above my right temple, so I stretched out on the couch to rest. As I lay there I noticed the scrap of paper on the end table with Jess's phone number. I picked it up and looked at it closely. After her name she had drawn a smiley face with hearts for eyes, and I found myself wondering why I hadn't called her. I originally planned to wait a day or two so I wouldn't seem too anxious, but now four days had passed. I really did want to call her, but had been so distracted by the story of Evelyn Welsh that I simply hadn't.

I put the slip of paper back on the end table and closed my eyes. As I rested, I mulled over the details of Evelyn's murder I had learned from the newspaper articles. The evidence against Neil Fischer was overwhelming. That, combined with his confession, left no doubt in my mind they had arrested and convicted the right person.

After admitting to the murder, Neil told the authorities he had disposed of Evelyn's body by dumping it in the Susquehanna River a few miles from where her clothes were found. After an exhaustive search of the river her body had not been recovered, however, and most of those involved with the investigation doubted whether Neil was telling the truth. But if that was the case, what was his reasoning behind it? I could understand that without a body it would have been more difficult to convict him, but he had already confessed to the murder. And now that he was in prison, what could he possibly have to lose by telling the world what he had done with her? He also didn't seem to have any animosity towards her or her family. He simply wouldn't explain why he did it.

I'm not sure why it bothered me so much. I'd read about things like this before, and while I always felt bad for the victims and their families, this really affected me. Maybe it was because I had stood right where it happened. Maybe it was because Evelyn seemed so young and innocent. Or maybe it was something else.

One thing I did know was that I wouldn't be satisfied until I talked to someone who knew more about it than anyone else. A quick phone call to the local police station told me that Detective Vaughn had retired several years ago, but still lived close by. After another call to the information line, I had his phone number.

CHAPTER 9

August 31, 1965

Charles Vaughn sat at his desk going over the notes from his interviews with Evelyn's friends, relatives, and co-workers. Three days earlier he received word that a bag of clothing had been found by one of the search teams covering a densely wooded area southwest of town. The items were brought into the police station and the detective stood by as Mr. and Mrs. Welsh examined them. They included a pair of white and yellow canvas sneakers, light blue capri-length denim pants, and a white cotton blouse, all heavily stained with soil and blood. Doris Welsh picked up the cotton blouse. As she lifted it to her face and held it against her cheek she broke down, her shoulders convulsing as she tried to speak.

"They're hers," was all she could say through the tears.

John placed his hand on his wife's shoulder and looked at the floor, saying nothing.

With the discovery and positive identification of the clothes, it now seemed very unlikely that Evelyn was still alive. Neil was nowhere to be found and all the evidence pointed to him as the perpetrator: his relationship with Evelyn, the bloody boot prints found at the crime scene, his ability to access the park after hours, and of course, his disappearance immediately afterwards.

The detective's thoughts were cut short by the ringing of his desk phone.

"Detective Vaughn here," he answered.

"Hello Detective. This is Chief Reinhart of the Watertown Police Department in New York."

"Uh, yes," Charles replied, somewhat confused. "How can I help you?"

"We have someone here I believe you're looking for."

"And who might that be?" he asked, suddenly feeling a glimmer of hope that Evelyn had been found alive.

"Neil Fischer. We picked him up this morning."

July 1, 1978

I sat in the den at Charles Vaughn's home and looked around. It was a simply furnished room that fit with the rest of the house, a small unassuming bungalow. Several pictures of the former detective with his fellow officers hung on the wall, along with framed citations and service awards he had received over the years. He lit a pipe and sat down in a dark brown leather chair with worn armrests.

"Thanks for taking the time to see me, Detective Vaughn," I said, settling into the seat across from him.

"You're welcome son. But there's no need to call me detective. No one does anymore. Charles will do just fine."

"Okay…Charles."

"So, I understand you have some questions about the Evelyn Welsh case."

"Yes sir."

"And this is for a journalism project for college?"

"Well, not exactly. I wasn't completely up front when I called yesterday and asked to meet with you. My interest is more personal than academic."

I went into detail about how I became interested in the case. I also recounted everything I had learned from the old newspaper articles. "I know it was a pretty open and shut case. But was there anything else you came across in your investigation that wasn't in the papers?"

"Of course there was. We had a number of different leads we were following up. In a case like this there's no shortage of people calling in with their ideas, and we need to look into them no matter how ridiculous they sound. One guy even suggested that John Welsh had ties to organized crime, and that we should consider the possibility that Evelyn's death may have been a professional hit. Another crackpot was convinced that Evelyn had really been abducted by aliens and taken away in a UFO, but for obvious reasons we didn't spend a lot of time following up on that one."

The former detective continued, "There wasn't much support for any of the alternate theories, even the more believable ones, and when Neil confessed there was little reason to pursue them any further. There was also a lot of pressure to wrap up the investigation and bring the case to trial. Everyone wanted justice for Evelyn."

"Can you tell me more about Evelyn? Mr. Sensenig told me there were rumors going around that she might not have been as innocent as she seemed. He also said something about her making some bad decisions."

Charles frowned.

"Oh, that."

"What was it?" I pressed.

"Well, I guess after this many years it won't matter that much if I tell you." He hesitated and then continued. "Some of her friends thought that Neil may have talked her into doing drugs, possibly heroin. One of her closest friends even claimed to have seen track marks on her arms, although her parents insisted they were just bruises."

"That's hard to believe. I mean, I didn't know her, but she didn't seem like someone that would do that. It wasn't mentioned in any of the newspaper articles I read either, at least not that I can recall."

"That's because John and Doris Welsh were able to keep it out of the papers, for the most part. They were very influential here in Hershey, and didn't want their daughter's reputation damaged in any way. They were even able to convince the police department to leave it out of the reports released to the public. It did eventually come out later and was mentioned in the Philadelphia and Baltimore papers, but not the local ones. No one around here wanted to believe it anyway, and we had no way of confirming whether it was even true."

"I see."

"Is there anything else you want to know about?"

"What about the murder weapon?" I asked.

"After his confession Neil admitted to stabbing her several times, which explained the amount of blood found at the crime scene. He said he disposed of the knife along with the body, but neither was ever found."

"Do you think that's significant?"

"Well, only because both would be important in

establishing a solid case against Neil. That's why his confession was so important. Without it, it would have been much more difficult to convict him."

"Do you have any idea why Neil never gave a motive for killing her?"

"Unfortunately, I don't."

"What about the body? Is there any reason to think he didn't really dispose of it in the river, and if not, why would he lie about it?

"I've asked myself those questions many times over the years. You seem like a bright young man. What do you think?"

I hesitated as I ran through some of the possible explanations in my head.

"I think maybe Neil just made a mistake…a terrible mistake. I don't think it was ever his plan to kill Evelyn, and that he was truly ashamed of what he had done and wasn't the monster everyone made him out to be. Maybe if they never found the body and saw what he had done, in a way he somehow wouldn't need to face up to it."

"Could be," replied Charles. "Or maybe he didn't want there to be an autopsy. A thorough examination of the body could have revealed more than he wanted anyone to know."

"Like the drug use?"

"Either that, or something else."

I paused as I thought about what he might be implying.

"Do you mean she could have been raped?"

"Who knows? It wouldn't be unusual in this type of situation. Even if their relationship was consensual, she was only sixteen."

I hadn't considered that possibility. But the detective had years of experience and a lot of time to think about this particular case over the past thirteen years. And it would certainly explain why Neil might not want there to be an autopsy.

I ended up spending several hours with Charles. By the time we finished, I realized he had been personally affected by Evelyn's death. Several times during our discussion his voice would trail off, and he seemed to be searching his memory for something that might help it all make sense.

CHAPTER 10

September 3, 1965

Neil Fischer sat alone in one of the interrogation rooms at the police station. The room was painted a drab gray and the only contents were a worn oak table and three chairs. Neil occupied a single chair on one side of the table, facing the two empty seats opposite him. A paper calendar hung on the wall advertising Campbelltown Motors, still showing the month of July 1965. He had been led into the room more than half an hour earlier and no one had entered since then. Neil was sure this was intentional, probably the first step in what would be a long process to put him on edge and begin to break him down. He steeled himself for what was to come and tried to look as nonchalant as possible.

Another fifteen minutes passed until the door swung

open and two men entered the room. The first to come in wore street clothes: a brown tweed jacket slightly frayed at the sleeves and tan chinos. The other was in uniform.

"Hello Mr. Fischer. I'm Detective Vaughn and this is Officer Harnish."

Neil looked at them but didn't speak. The detective and his associate pulled out the two empty chairs and sat down.

"I'll get right to the point Neil. Where is Evelyn Welsh and how are you involved?"

Neil stared at them. "So, you're not going to tell me I'm allowed to make a phone call? Maybe I want to talk to my lawyer."

"Sure," answered Detective Vaughn with a sigh. "Who's your attorney? We'll get him on the phone for you."

"Do I look like someone who would have an attorney?" mocked Neil.

"Legal representation can be provided for you if you would like it."

"Nope, I'm good."

The detective could see how this was going to go.

"Okay then, let's try this again. Where is Evelyn Welsh and how are you involved?"

"I have no idea what you're talking about."

"Sure you do. Evelyn went missing over a week ago, and you disappeared at exactly the same time. We both know it's not a coincidence."

Charles was careful not to mention anything about the crime scene or any details that weren't already provided in the news, hoping to trip him up at some point during the conversation.

"Sorry, I can't help you."

"You were close friends with her, weren't you?"

"I knew her."

"Well, you don't seem very upset that she's missing," said the detective, trying to push Neil.

"Should I be? Besides, we really weren't that close. It's not like she was my girlfriend or anything…she wasn't my type. You know, she was a little too straight-laced for me."

"From what I've heard you were more than just friends. A number of people have told me you were spending a lot of time together."

"People say a lot of things. It doesn't mean they're true."

Charles watched Neil closely as he questioned him. Based on what he learned from his interviews over the past week the detective already knew Neil was lying about his relationship with Evelyn, but that wasn't why he was asking. There was another reason. The detective could tell, almost without fail, when someone wasn't being truthful. Body language such as sitting too far up on the edge of the seat might indicate a person was nervous about the answer he was giving, while appearing overly relaxed could mean he was trying too hard to hide his guilt. Sitting in a defensive position, crossing their arms, or not making direct eye contact when giving answers were also indications. Charles had observed none of those signs during the interview, which just confirmed the detective's suspicions. Neil was an experienced liar.

"Were you attracted to her?" the detective continued.

"What kind of a question is that?"

"A standard one."

"She was kind of pretty, if that's what you mean. I'm sure anyone would tell you that."

Charles nodded as Neil answered, then said "You know, it's also interesting that you've been using the past tense to describe her. Any particular reason?"

"Only because you did first."

July 4, 1978:

Since the Independence Day holiday fell on a Tuesday, Hall Construction shut down operations on both July 3rd and July 4th that summer. Mr. Hall was fiercely patriotic and felt that it was important that his employees not only had time to spend with their families, but also time to reflect on the sacrifices made by many Americans over the years. The holiday had a special meaning to him, having served in Vietnam during the height of the conflict in the late 1960s. According to Jeff, his dad rarely talked about his experiences there. One thing he did say was that even though he often questioned the reasons he was there, he was proud to have stood and fought beside some of the finest men he had ever met, many of whom did not return.

Mr. Hall started his construction business soon after his last tour of duty, mostly because there were few jobs waiting for men like him returning from the war. The tenacity he learned from serving there had contributed to the success of his business, and whenever possible he made it a point to hire veterans or young men who had lost their fathers in the jungles of Southeast Asia.

All of that seemed very distant now, as Jeff and I sat in our lawn chairs in his backyard. Mr. Hall stood in front of the charcoal grill with a metal spatula in one hand and a cold Michelob in the other, while Mrs. Hall carried a tray of hamburger rolls and condiments to the picnic table. As she walked past him she reminded him not to burn them like the last time, and he took advantage of the fact that her hands were full and smacked her rear end with the spatula.

"Now you stop that Mr. Hall," she said with feigned anger. "You'll get grease on my new sun dress!"

I laughed to myself as I watched the two of them together. Jeff was lucky, as I was, to have parents that cared deeply for one another and enjoyed each other's company.

"So where did you get to on Saturday?" asked Jeff. "I stopped by to see if you wanted to shoot some baskets, but you were gone most of the day."

I hesitated at first, but then figured that Jeff was probably the one person I could tell.

"I went to see Charles Vaughn, the detective that investigated Evelyn Welsh's murder."

"You did what?"

"You heard me. I went to see Charles Vaughn."

"But why would you do that?"

"I'm not sure, exactly. Ever since Hank told me about what happened I can't seem to get her off my mind."

"Holy crap, Chad," responded Jeff, "Most guys obsess about girls that are still alive, not ones that have been dead for years."

"I know, but I just keep feeling like she won't be at peace until her remains are found. I know the truth is out there, and someone should try to find it out."

"I know what you're saying Chad, but she's dead. Why does it matter whether her body is buried in a cemetery or somewhere else? And why is the truth about this, and everything else, always so important to you?"

Jeff had a good point. I didn't really know why I cared so much about Evelyn. But I did know why the truth was important to me. There were several different experiences in my life that had contributed to it, but one particular instance stood out. I tried my best to explain it to Jeff.

When I was ten years old, there was a family that lived next door to us. Their son, Travis, was one of my best friends at the time. His family life wasn't the greatest though. The dad was an alcoholic and had a really bad temper. And it didn't matter whether he was drunk or sober, the littlest thing would set him off. Because of that, Travis just tried to keep his head down and be as invisible as possible around their dad. But Travis really looked up to his older brother, Jason, who was around seventeen at the time. Even though Jason thought his little brother was a nuisance and told him so regularly, Travis would still do anything for him, hoping to get from him what he never got from their father.

One night, after their dad passed out on the couch after a day of boozing, Jason stole the keys to his new Pontiac GTO and took it out for a ride. Of course, he ended up putting a huge scratch down the side of the car from the front quarter panel to the middle of the door. But when Jason got home, he just put the keys back and never said a word to anyone. Travis knew what had happened though.

The next morning when their dad had sobered up, he saw the car and went ballistic. I was out in the front yard when he called Jason and Travis out to the driveway and grilled them about how it had happened. Jason wouldn't admit to it, and his dad was about to lay into him when Travis stepped up and took the blame for it. He made up a story about how we were riding bike in the driveway and he wasn't being careful and scratched it.

His dad looked at me and asked if it was true, but I didn't say anything. Then he looked at Jason and asked the same thing. Jason just nodded in agreement. Finally, he turned back to Travis and said, "I always knew you were worthless."

From that point forward there was a change in Travis. He withdrew into himself even more than before, and rarely came outside to play after that. Within months his dad lost his job, the house, and his beloved GTO. Their family ended up moving away so he could find work, and I never saw Travis again. For years when I thought back on it, I'd get angry that Jason wasn't man enough to admit he did it. But I was even more upset at myself for not saying anything. It would have been such a small thing for me to speak up and tell him what really happened, but I didn't.

"I see what you're saying," replied Jeff. "But here's the thing. Sometimes it's also better not to know the truth. It certainly would have been better if Travis didn't know how his dad really felt about him."

Jeff had a good point, and in the end, I guess that's the problem with the truth. Even though it brings freedom to those who look hard enough to find it, it can also be painful.

"Maybe you're right," I replied, "but it still doesn't change how I feel about Evelyn."

"Well, if you want my advice, you should concentrate less on Evelyn Welsh and more on Jessie Sanders. She has way more to offer," said Jeff with a wink.

CHAPTER 11

September 5, 1965

Charles Vaughn knew they wouldn't be able to detain Neil much longer without pressing charges. They did have some leeway since he had refused an attorney, who would have obtained a writ of habeas corpus forcing them to either file charges or release him. Although all the evidence pointed to him as the perpetrator, most of it was circumstantial. Even the footprints found at the scene weren't conclusive since his boots could not be located and they were a common brand of work shoes. Also, since Evelyn's body had not been found, it was still officially a missing persons case. Neil would most likely be free by that afternoon.

They had questioned Neil several times since he was brought in, but each time they failed to trip him up or get any additional information that was helpful. He would just antagonize and frustrate them, knowing just how much to say and no more. Charles was convinced they would not be able to break Neil or even get him to admit to anything that would incriminate him. Consequently, Detective Vaughn was somewhat surprised when Neil requested to talk to him again that morning.

He was led back into the same room as before and took the seat across from Charles. Officer Harnish leaned against the wall next to him, looking annoyed. As he sat down, Neil glanced at the calendar on the wall that still showed the wrong month.

"You know, you should really change that thing. I'm starting to lose track of how long I've been here. Unless that was part of your plan--"

"Listen Neil," the detective interrupted, "If you're just going to be belligerent like you have every other time we've sat here, you're going right back to your holding cell. I'm not in the mood for any more of your bullshit."

"I understand," replied Neil.

"So, just what is it you wanted to talk about?"

"There's something I need to tell you."

"And what is that?"

Neil looked directly at him with a look of determination.

"I did it."

"Did what?"

"I killed her. I killed Evelyn."

July 8, 1978

Another Saturday morning had arrived, and I rolled out of bed. I looked around desperately for some clothes to wear, since my laundry was one of the many things that had taken a back seat over the past week. After rummaging through the piles, I settled on a wrinkled pair of shorts and a Ramones t-shirt that still smelled reasonably clean.

The night after the Hall's Fourth of July cookout, I decided to take Jeff's advice and finally called Jess. She was a little surprised to hear from me after so much time had passed, and told me I really knew how to play it cool. I assured her I was anything but cool, and explained that a busy work schedule and a few personal things I had going on were the only reasons I hadn't called sooner. She seemed okay with my explanation, and we ended up talking for several hours. I wasn't nearly as nervous talking to her on the phone as I was in person, but that was probably because I couldn't see her green-brown eyes looking back at me or see her flip her hair back when she laughed.

Jess told me about her family, and especially the close relationship she had with her younger brother. He had been a surprise for her parents, coming along eleven years after her, and was born with developmental disabilities. Although his condition required so much of her family's attention, Jess loved him beyond words. As a result, she planned to become a teacher after she graduated and work with children with special needs. She was originally planning to enroll at a State university back home in Maryland and didn't think she'd be able to afford the tuition of a private institution like Franklin and Marshall College. But the application essay she had written about her brother and how he had inspired her must have caught the attention of someone in the admissions office. Jess ended up not only getting accepted, but also offered enough scholarship money to make it possible for her to attend there. I told myself I should thank the entire admissions staff at F&M, and her brother, if I ever met him.

I briefly considered telling Jess what the personal things were that had been taking up so much of my time, but then thought better of it. I wasn't sure what she'd think about my interest in a young girl's murder from thirteen years ago, and certainly didn't want to ruin my chances with her before things even got started. And although it was great to finally talk to Jess again, I still wasn't ready to give up on Evelyn. In fact, my plans for the day once again centered around her.

The wooded area where Evelyn's clothing had been found years ago was part of the Pennsylvania State Game Lands No. 246. The property was made up of over 240 acres surrounding a small mountain known as Round Top to the residents who lived nearby. From my conversations with Charles Vaughn, I knew the specific location could most easily be reached from a small gravel parking area just off Roundtop Road, a local road that ran southwest along the base of the mountain before heading towards Middletown, PA and the Susquehanna River.

I had managed to convince Jeff it would be a nice day for a hike, and we stood at a trailhead next to the parking area. After looking over a topographic map I copied from the library, we headed east on a trail climbing towards the top of the mountain. I'm not sure what I thought I would find that day. So much time had passed since Evelyn's death, and the area had been combed over by dozens of volunteers and law enforcement personnel during the search. Still, I felt it was important to see the place. Other than the Gold Nugget, it was the only location where any actual evidence of the young girl's murder had been discovered.

We covered less than a mile of ground before we came to the start of a small wash that started just off the trail and ran down the side of the ridge. I rechecked the map to be sure we were at the right spot, then pushed my way through a large stand of brush along the trail.

"Uh, where are you going?" asked Jeff. "Don't tell me you have to take a leak already?"

"No, I just want to look for something."

As I emerged from the other side of the brush I could see further down the hillside along the wash. A lone Red Oak tree stood about forty feet downslope of the trail, dwarfing the other Tulip Poplars and White Pines growing on the side of the mountain.

"I think that's it," I said to Jeff.

"That's what?"

"It's the Red Oak tree. The plastic bag with Evelyn's clothes was found near the base of that tree."

"Evelyn?" asked Jeff.

"Evelyn Welsh."

"I know who you mean. Please don't tell me you dragged me out here to look for clues to a murder that was solved years ago. It's bad enough you went to the library to read up on this, and even worse that you went to see that detective. You really are going off the deep end, you know."

I started to feel a little ridiculous. Maybe Jeff was right.

"I know. But I just can't seem to let this go, and I'm not sure why. It still really bothers me that Evelyn's body was never found."

"I guess I can understand that," said Jeff. "It's terrible what happened to her, but what do you think you could possibly figure out that no one else has."

Once again, I didn't have an answer.

We picked our way down to the tree, and sat down on some rocks next to it, catching our breath. It was silent except for a few birds chirping nearby and a light breeze blowing through the tree canopy. A minute passed until Jeff spoke.

"You know, he really picked a bad spot to hide the evidence."

"What do you mean?"

"Well, look at all the boulders around here. If I was going to hide something, I'd pick a spot where it was a lot easier, that's for sure. You could barely dig six inches down here without hitting a rock, and I'd want to bury it as deep as I could. And why pick a spot so close to the trail? It was only a matter of time until someone found it."

I looked at Jeff, trying to think of a reason.

"I'm sure he was in a hurry. He could have been afraid they were going to catch up to him."

"Yeah, but if that's the case why even take the time to drive somewhere else to get rid of her clothes? Why not just leave them with her?" He paused. "Unless…"

"Unless he wanted them to be found," I answered.

"Of course," said Jeff. "Maybe he wanted to throw off the authorities. Once her things were found here I'm sure the search efforts would have been concentrated in this area more than the others. He could have been trying to lead them away from where he really hid the body."

I thought about it for a second. "That would explain the bill of sale they found in the parking area with Neil's name on it. I don't think he would have been careless enough to drop something like that and not pick it up. And there were a number of people close to the case that thought Neil was lying about dumping her body in the river. These woods are pretty much on a direct line between Hershey and Falmouth, the spot on the Susquehanna where Neil supposedly got rid of her. Picking this location to leave some evidence would have helped reinforce his story."

"Or he could have just been taunting them," added Jeff. "From what you've said, Neil didn't have much respect for authority. It's possible he was giving them just enough to make them think they were getting close, when he knew they'd never find her."

"That's pretty sadistic."

"So is killing a 16-year-old girl."

CHAPTER 12

July 14, 1965

Evelyn sat on the sofa in Neil's apartment, looking nervous. He walked around the room closing the blinds and, when he had pulled the last of them shut, turned off all the lights except for a small lamp on the end table. As Neil sat down next to her, she looked up and her eyes met his.

"Are you sure you're ready to do this?" he asked.

"Yes, I'm sure I'm ready."

"Okay, I just don't want to force you into anything you don't want to do."

"No, it's fine. And I'm sorry about the other night…I shouldn't have reacted the way I did," she assured him. "Just be careful. I don't want it to hurt."

Neil looked at her closely.

"Do you trust me?"

"Of course I do," was her answer.

Evelyn closed her eyes and tried to relax as Neil reached over, lifted her arm, and placed it in his lap. He grabbed a long rubber strip from the coffee table and gently wrapped it around her upper arm, making sure the tourniquet was just tight enough to increase her blood pressure without entirely cutting off the flow of blood. Then he looked over the inside of her arm, found a good vein, and reached for the needle on the table.

"Tell me when you're going to do it, because I don't want to watch," said Evelyn nervously.

"Ok, here it goes."

As he stuck the needle into her soft inner arm she winced slightly from the pain, but within seconds she relaxed completely.

July 12, 1978

The Safe Harbor Dam was built across the lower Susquehanna River in the early 1930s. It was one of several public Depression Era hydroelectric projects, and the turbines in the power plant at the eastern end of the dam had supplied electricity for the Pennsylvania Railroad as it transitioned out of the steam era. The dam spanned the entire river, forming the long and shallow Lake Clarke as a result.

On this particular morning, the chief engineer for the Safe Harbor Hydroelectric Station walked slowly along the top of the concrete dam breast at the power plant. Three days of heavy rain across the central portion of the state had cleared the river banks of loose debris, which was now piled up against the large intake screens protecting the turbines. His maintenance crews would be working all morning to clear the screens, and he was just finishing his inspection to make sure that none of them had been damaged by the larger limbs that had washed downstream.

Everything appeared to be in good working order, and as he finished he looked into the pool at the water's edge just beyond the last intake screen. One of his crew members was wading in the shallow water, picking up some smaller debris and accumulated trash. The worker stopped and seemed to be staring at a collection of objects resting on the silty bottom. They were similar in size to the small branches he had been picking up, but appeared much lighter in color, almost as if they had been bleached white.

"Hey boss!" he called up to the engineer.

"What is it?"

"I think you'd better take a look at this."

On most days, Jeff went to the job site early to help his dad plan the day's work. This morning was different, however, since he was recovering from a late night out with Cheryl. As I rode in the passenger seat of his truck, I did what any good friend would do and pressed him for the details.

"So, you got in pretty late last night. That must be a good sign."

"Yeah, I guess so. Cheryl's really a great girl. You know, she's different than most of the women I've been with."

"So, you're not getting anywhere?"

"Not even close."

I laughed at the thought of Jeff finally going after someone with high standards. "Well, there must be something about her you really like. Normally you would have bailed by now."

He sighed. "I know. This is new territory for me. I just hope this doesn't mean I'm maturing or anything like that."

Jeff fiddled with the radio as we talked, passing over my favorite Rolling Stones song. Since I had met Jeff the previous September, the only real disagreement I could remember having was whether or not *Beast of Burden* was one of the best songs ever written. I felt it clearly was, but it didn't surprise me when he skipped over it.

He continued to flip through the stations.

"The Dow Jones was up 3.64 points to close at 824.93 in a day of light trading...what appear to be several human bones were found yesterday in the Lake Clarke area of the Susquehanna River...Steve Carlton will go up against Phil Niekro in Friday's game at...."

"Wait, go back!" I shouted.

"Go back where?" asked Jeff, glancing into his rearview mirror and then at me.

"Back to that last station! They were saying something about bones being found."

I pushed his hand out of the way and tuned the radio to the local news station he had passed over.

"The County Coroner and law enforcement personnel will be examining them over the next several days in an attempt to identify the victim. Based on the condition of the bones it appears they had been in the river for a long time, and matching them to any missing persons or known drowning victims may prove to be difficult. WTTF-FM public radio will continue to provide updates as they become available."

Jeff and I looked at each other.

"Do you think they could be Evelyn's?" he asked.

I could almost sense he was becoming as interested as I was in finding out what had happened to her.

"I don't know. Detective Vaughn said that Neil claimed to have dumped her body just south of Falmouth. They had dive teams searching and boats dragging the bottom from there all the way down to Safe Harbor. The search went on for over a week, but that's still probably twenty miles of river they had to cover. I guess it's possible they could have just missed her."

Given the recent news, I found it hard to concentrate on work that day. I had grabbed a small transistor radio from the glove compartment in Jeff's truck, and kept it tuned to WITF hoping to hear an update. Nothing more significant was revealed that day, but several experts were interviewed on the subject.

I learned that the Susquehanna River was a deceptively dangerous body of water. It was shallow and slow-moving at most spots, giving swimmers and waders a false sense of safety. At other locations where the river narrowed slightly or the bottom contour changed, the velocity increased enough to catch an unsuspecting person off guard and, as a result, hundreds of people had drowned there over the years.

A representative from the County Coroner's office

also talked about the process used to identify bodies or other remains found in the river. Apparently the rate of decay could vary significantly depending on a number of factors such as the temperature of the water and whether the body surfaced at all. In some cases, the victim was unrecognizable after only two days in the water and identification had be done based on articles of clothing or jewelry found on the body, or by examining, scars, tattoos, or fingerprints. If a body wasn't recovered after about a year in the water, the flesh would be completely eaten away, and the job became much more difficult. In those cases, they could only rely on bone size measurements, dental records, or skeletal deformities to identify the victim.

Another day passed without any new information. I found myself hoping the bones belonged to Evelyn, not only because it would bring closure to her case, but also so I could stop dwelling on the whole thing and have a more normal existence.

The following evening, as Jeff and I sat in his family room watching the television, the report we were waiting for finally came.

'Less than an hour ago the Lancaster County Coroner's office announced that a positive identification has been made regarding the bones found at Safe Harbor Dam earlier this week. The conclusion

was reached early this morning based on evidence of a healed prior fracture of a tibia bone that was recovered, but a public announcement was delayed until the family could be notified. According to information provided to WGAL-TV 8, the remains were identified as those of Anthony Hurst, a 12-year-old boy missing since June 23, 1976 when his grandfather's boat capsized while fishing. The incident occurred just north of the Veteran's Memorial Bridge near Wrightsville, PA and..."

Jeff switched off the television. "Sorry, man."

"That's okay. I knew it was a long shot anyway."

"Maybe someday they'll find her."

I thought about it for a while, then answered.

"No they won't. At least not in the river."

"What makes you say that?"

"Because that's not where he got rid of her body. I just know it."

CHAPTER 13

October 11, 1965

Neil stood in the packed court room facing the Judge. The state-assigned public defender had done his best trying to negotiate a deal with the District Attorney on Neil's behalf, but Neil's refusal to provide a motive or provide any additional information regarding the location of Evelyn's remains left him with little bargaining power. The District Attorney intended to seek a first-degree murder charge, even though he recognized there was a lack of evidence that it had been planned. Based on Neil's relationship with the victim, the popular opinion was that it was a crime of passion and, although tragic, had not been premeditated. Neil continued to maintain he had disposed her body in the Susquehanna River and offered no other explanation, and the case appeared to be headed to trial. With Neil's confession on the record, the District Attorney was confident that a jury would return a guilty verdict. However, in a surprise turn of events intended to prevent the Welsh family from enduring the emotional pain of a trial, the District Attorney agreed to accept the plea of third-degree murder and slightly reduced sentence presented by the public defender. The clerk opened the proceedings.

"Court is now in session, the Honorable Judge Stephen Bowman presiding."

Judge Bowman addressed Neil. "In the matter of the Commonwealth of Pennsylvania vs. Neil Fischer, how do you plead?"

Neil looked at him without emotion and answered, "Guilty, your Honor."

"Have you reached a settlement, Counsel?"

"Yes, your Honor," answered the District Attorney. "The people have agreed to a sentence of fifteen to thirty-five years in prison, with the possibility of parole after twenty years."

The judge turned his attention back to Neil.

"Mr. Fischer, are you aware that by pleading guilty you give up the right to a trial by a jury of your peers?"

"Yes, your Honor."

"And do you willingly give up that right?"

"Yes, I do."

"And do you understand that are also waiving your right against self-incrimination and your right to confront and cross-examine your accusers?"

"Yes, your Honor."

"Has your decision been made under duress or do you feel you've been forced to accept this settlement."

"No."

Judge Bowman looked closely over his notes regarding the case before continuing.

"Mr. Fischer, while the plea bargain agreement and suggested sentencing are within the appropriate guidelines for a crime of this nature, I'm extremely concerned about your level of cooperation with regard to this case. Your refusal to reveal your motive or the location of Evelyn's remains leaves her family without the closure that is vitally important as they grieve the loss of their daughter. I want to give you one last opportunity to make the right decision about this, so I'm going to ask you once more to reconsider your silence on this matter. Where is Evelyn Welsh?"

A hush fell across the court room as the Judge waited for Neil's response.

"I'm sorry your honor, but I refuse to answer that."

The Judge frowned.

"Very well, Mr. Fischer. I'm willing to accept the plea of murder in the third degree, but in light of your decision I feel I have no choice but to reject the reduced sentencing as presented. You are hereby sentenced to the maximum term of twenty to forty years in prison minus time already served, without the possibility of parole."

Later that day, two inmates sat on a bench in the prison yard. At first appearances it was a typical day, the same as the previous days and the same as many more to come. But today the shorter of the two prisoners looked around slowly, taking note of where each of the guards were and which direction they were facing. The other inmate leaned back on the bench as if he was bored. He was a large muscular man of about forty years of age with a bushy mustache and thin dark hair. The man, who was serving two life sentences, was known as The Dean to the other inmates. He had earned the nickname due to his reputation as an enforcer within the prison. Most often he was referred to as simply Dean.

"Is everything still on schedule?" asked Dean.

"Yeah. He came in about an hour ago."

"Has he been processed yet?"

"No, but the word is they should be finishing up soon."

"Good. Do you have it?"

"I've got it right here. I had a little trouble with the new guard, but I told him it was for you. It's not my best work, but it should do the job."

When the shorter one was convinced that no one was watching, he pulled an object from his pants and put it on the seat between them. Dean placed his hand over the object, waited a few seconds, then slid it quickly into the front of his pants where it could be held in place by the elastic waist band of his briefs. The two continued to talk for several minutes until the buzzer rang signaling the end of free time, then stood up and walked to the door that would take them back to their respective cell blocks.

At that same time, in the interior of the prison, Neil Fischer was being led down a hallway by two guards. He had been transferred to the facility following his sentencing and had just been processed to become a permanent resident. The shackles that bound his feet for the van ride to the prison had been removed, but his wrists remained cuffed together. Although the guards had been instructed to take him directly to Cell Number 105, which would become his permanent home, they stopped abruptly outside an isolated room often used for solitary confinement. Neil was instructed to enter the room alone, and the door closed behind him. Shortly afterwards, another guard led Dean down the same hallway. As they reached the room, he stopped and nodded at the other two guards. They quickly opened the door, and allowed Dean to step in. As he entered the confinement room, he reached into the front of his pants and retrieved a crudely fashioned set of brass knuckles and slid them onto his right hand.

Neil had much to learn about prison, but he knew enough to realize he was in trouble as soon as he was left in the room by himself. He looked up as the other inmate entered and walked directly towards him. Instinctively, he raised his cuffed hands to protect his face, but the first blow connected with his ribs, making a sickening crunch. Neil doubled over. The next hit, a roundhouse swing, nailed him squarely in the side of the face, knocking him to the floor. His cheek split open immediately, and blood ran down his face into the corner of his mouth, bringing with it the familiar copper taste Neil had experienced so often before. The pain was excruciating, and he knew he wouldn't last much longer unless he acted quickly. He also knew that his reputation, and how he would be treated by the other prisoners in the future, would largely be determined by what happened in that room.

As his assailant came towards him to continue the beating, his left foot stepped on the floor between Neil's arms. Neil saw his opportunity and yanked his cuffed hands quickly towards him, taking Dean's leg out from under him and knocking him off balance. He fell to the floor and Neil lunged towards him. The handcuffs prevented him from taking a full swing, so he struck Dean's jaw with the heel of his hand, putting all of his body weight behind it. Neil felt the man's jaw dislocate as he hit it. It was enough to stop him momentarily, and Neil swung around behind him, pulling the chain from his handcuffs against the man's throat. Dean reached up to pull the chain away, but Neil yanked it tighter and tighter against his windpipe, choking him. His arms flailed helplessly, striking at Neil but failing to make any solid contact.

At that moment the three guards burst into the room, pulling the two apart. Had they chosen to wait much longer, Dean would have been dead. As it was, it would be some time until he would be able to speak or eat solid food. Neil hadn't fared much better, but he had done his best to send the message that he was not going to be an easy target.

Unfortunately for him, it would take much more than that. There would always be someone else waiting for their chance to make him pay for what he had done to young Evelyn Welsh.

July 15, 1978

It was still dark when I dragged myself out of bed, and would be for at least another half an hour. Jess and I had talked on the phone several times over the past two weeks, and things seemed to being going pretty well with her. In fact, she had invited me to come see her that weekend. Her little brother, Joey, was participating in his first Special Olympics meet in Rockville, Maryland. The Special Olympics had its beginnings in the neighboring town of Potomac about fifteen years earlier, when Eunice Kennedy Shriver started a day camp at her home for children with intellectual disabilities. Ms. Shriver's articles written for the Washington Post at that time had done much to change peoples' attitudes about individuals with disabilities, and the program had been gaining popularity ever since.

Jess had volunteered to help plan and run the event and, since that would occupy much of her time, she asked if I would be willing to be Joey's buddy for the day. I was glad she thought of me and that she would trust me enough to look after her younger brother. In fact, I told her so soon after I arrived that morning.

"I'm really glad you could come," she said. "But to be honest, Joey doesn't really need a buddy. He's pretty good at taking care of himself."

I looked at her questioningly.

"I really just asked you here to see if you pass the Joey test," she said with a smile. "If he doesn't like you, there's no need for this relationship to go any further." Then she winked at me and walked away.

I was suddenly very nervous about meeting her brother. But I was also encouraged that she described whatever it was that we had as a "relationship". She came back a few minutes later holding Joey's hand.

"Joey, this is Chad. He's a friend of mine and he's going to be hanging out with you today."

I don't think I ever saw a kid smile that big before. "Hi Chad," he said enthusiastically, "Stick with me. I'll make sure you don't get lost."

"See what I mean?" said Jess. "He thinks you're the one that needs to be watched."

"I hope you're strong Chad," Joey continued, "Because I'm going to win a lot of medals today and you're going to need to carry them."

I laughed and answered, "I think I can handle that."

Joey and I had a great time together that day. He had an unbridled enthusiasm, and gave his all in every event.

He was also the most positive kid I had ever met, and I knew there was a lot I could learn from him. As an only child I had occasionally wondered what it would be like to have a brother, but I had never pictured having one like Joey. I could see why Jess was so fond of him.

Around mid-day we took a break, and Joey and I sat under a tree eating our bagged lunches. As he devoured his ham sandwich, I looked across the field and caught a glimpse of Jess talking to some of the other volunteers. In one respect, I still thought of her as the beautiful, unattainable woman I had been admiring from a distance the entire school year, but I was also beginning to see her as something else. She was kind and down-to-earth, and I was starting to feel like I might actually have a chance with her.

"So, Joey, has your sister had any serious boyfriends?"

I figured it wouldn't hurt to ask.

"Why? Do you want her to be your girlfriend?" he answered and started to laugh.

I should have known he'd see right through me.

"I was just wondering," I said, backing off a little.

"She had one before. He was nice to me, but I don't think he was very nice to her. Jess always said he was eggo-tistical and shelf-centered. I don't know what either of those things mean, but I don't think they're very good."

"No, they're not. I'm sorry to hear that."

"Yeah, but they broke up. I think it was at least two years ago. She hasn't brought anyone around since then."

"Really?" I asked.

"Yeah, until now." He smiled at me and pushed his glasses further up on his nose.

"Well, I'm glad she did," I told him, "I wouldn't have met you otherwise."

"Me too, Chad. We're friends now."

As things wrapped up later that afternoon, I found myself wishing the day could be longer. I could tell Joey was running out of steam though, and to be honest, I was beginning to feel a bit tired myself. When it was over I said goodbye to him, and he gave me a bone crushing hug. Afterwards, Jess walked with me to my car.

"Thanks for being here for him today," she said, "It meant a lot to me, and I could tell he really liked hanging out with you."

"Does that mean I passed?" I asked as I slid into the front seat of my car.

She looked at me with amusement.

"Chad, I was just kidding about that. It wasn't really a test."

"It wasn't?"

"No. Joey loves everybody."

I glanced up at her and she leaned through the open window and gave me a kiss on the cheek. As she did, her hair fell across my face and I could smell the faint scent of strawberry.

"Call me soon," she said.

I promised her I would, then backed out of my parking spot to begin the two-hour drive home.

CHAPTER 14

April 7, 1967

The guard sitting in the corner of the prison visitation room yawned and looked at his watch. A round of the flu had been circulating through the prison staff, and he had been working overtime to cover for the other guards. Only two hours to go, he thought, and his shift would be over. As he looked over the prisoners in the room, his gaze fell on Neil Fischer and the woman seated across from him. Neil had been in prison for almost eighteen months and the woman had visited him several times, but this was the first time the guard had taken notice of her. She had long brown hair that fell down over her shoulders, and wore a smart-looking taupe jacket and matching skirt. The woman was attractive, but in a plain sort of way, and nothing about her, from her hair style to her clothing, called attention to herself. She's probably a librarian or a school teacher, he thought as he stood up to stretch his legs.

The two had been talking for nearly an hour, and the guard began to wonder who the woman might be and what reason she could have for visiting a convicted murderer. They didn't appear to be discussing anything very important, but the woman also didn't seem to be in any particular hurry to leave. He inched closer so he could listen in on their conversation, partially out of curiosity, and partially out of boredom.

As he made his way over the woman stood up to leave, and all he heard were the last few words of the conversation.

"When will you be in again?" asked Neil.

"Work is going to be really busy this month, but I'll be back in a few weeks."

"All right."

"Take care of yourself Neil," said the woman.

"Okay Sis, thanks for coming. And if you happen to run into Dad, could you give him a message for me?"

The woman appeared confused.

"Sure, what is it?" she asked.

"Tell him he should stop by sometime. I'm sure he'd like it here."

She laughed quietly to herself and walked out of the room.

July 22, 1978

My visit with Charles Vaughn and trip to the State Game Lands with Jeff had provided few answers and just raised more questions. The conclusion that the bones discovered at Safe Harbor dam were not Evelyn's had also frustrated me, but even before the announcement was made there was something deep inside of me that told me they wouldn't be hers.

It was clear that I really had become obsessed with Evelyn and what happened to her that summer in 1965. I knew I could never bring her back, but I felt if I could just find out where her remains were, I could somehow bring a measure of peace to her and those who knew her. I knew it might be a mistake, but I needed to talk to the one person who knew where she was.

Neil Fischer was incarcerated at the State Correctional Institution at Graterford, a maximum-security prison located about thirty miles northwest of Philadelphia. I looked around the visitation room as I waited for them to bring Neil in. A middle aged woman sat in a chair a few feet away, talking to her husband through the window that separated the visitors from the inmates. Her fingers reached up to touch her husband's hand through the safety glass as they spoke. A boy that looked to be about five years old played with his toy Hot Wheels cars on the floor nearby. I wondered what the man had done to end up in prison and how long he had been separated from his family. I also wondered if the boy had any memories of his father outside of that room.

Fifteen minutes had passed since I had taken my seat, and it occurred to me that Neil may not even agree to see me. On the other hand, I was sure he didn't get many visitors and might welcome the change in routine. A few minutes later a door opened, and the guard escorted a man who appeared to be in his forties to the seat across from me. I wasn't sure what I expected him to look like. I had seen pictures of him in the old newspaper articles and had expected him to have aged since then, but I wasn't really prepared for what I saw. Thirteen years in prison had taken its toll on Neil Fischer. He had aged, but he also bore the scars of the numerous beatings he had taken since his conviction. The prison population was not particularly kind to inmates who harmed children or innocent young people, and Neil was no exception.

"I don't get many visitors," he said as he sat down. "Do I know you?"

"No," I replied. "My name is Chad Anderson."

"Well hello, Chad Anderson. What brings you to the Graterford Hilton?"

"I came here to ask you some questions."

"About what?"

"About Evelyn Welsh."

Neil was quick to answer. "Well, you wasted your time. I said everything I had to say thirteen years ago."

"I'm not asking for a lot of your time, I'm just curious about a few things."

"Sorry kid. I'll talk about anything you want… just not Evelyn Welsh."

I considered changing the subject, but after making the long drive there I decided I had nothing to lose and pressed him further.

"Listen, I know you didn't dump her in the river. If you had, she would have been found by now. Why won't you tell anyone where she's buried?"

Obviously, I didn't know for sure whether she had actually been buried somewhere or whether he had disposed of the body in some other way. But I naively thought I might be able to get him to slip up and possibly reveal something he hadn't given up before.

Neil wasn't biting.

"Okay, if you're not going to answer that, at least tell

me why you left her clothes where they were sure to be found."

"What are you, some kind of junior detective?"

"No," I answered, "just someone who wants to know the truth."

He looked at me for a moment, then signaled to the guard that he was finished.

"Hold on," I pleaded. "It's not like you have anywhere to be."

"Listen, there's a lot of things I don't have control of around here. But I can still decide who I talk to and who I don't."

Neil stood up and walked out.

As I was escorted back through the corridor leading to the visitation room, I felt dejected and frustrated that I had learned nothing more. In hindsight, I wasn't sure why I even thought it might turn out any different. If no one else had gotten Neil to talk since 1965, what made me think that I could? I thanked the staff person at the front desk as I signed out.

"That was a short visit," she said, "I guess Neil wasn't up for a conversation."

"Apparently not," I replied.

I looked at the clock and listed my departure time on the sheet. As I wrote I glanced down over the list of visitors who had signed in and out, and a thought occurred to me.

"Does anyone else ever come to see him?" I asked.

"No, not really. I've been working here for over eight years, and the only person I ever remember coming to see him is his sister. She used to come pretty regularly the first few years, but then the visits became fewer and further between until they stopped entirely."

"How long do you think it's been since the last time she came?"

"At least three years, maybe four."

"Did they have a falling out or something?" I asked.

"I'm not sure. All I know is she stopped coming around."

"All right, thank you," I told her and walked out.

CHAPTER 15

July 24, 1978

It was a Monday afternoon when the Gold Nugget finally came down. Hank sat at the controls of a large track hoe, and I stood at a safe distance with the other workers as the CAT reached upward and tore at the façade of the building. The fake store fronts peeled easily off the wooden frame and, once they were down, Hank went to work on the roof. The old trusses splintered under the weight of the bucket, and by the middle of the afternoon the Gold Nugget was reduced to an unrecognizable pile of broken timbers. I continued to watch as a pair of bulldozers pushed the debris to the side so they could be loaded into a tri-axle dump truck waiting nearby. If any clues to Evelyn's death still remained in the building, they were now lost forever.

Jeff and I spent the next hour gathering up the remnants of lumber that had been missed by the bulldozers. As we picked through them and cleared the site to allow work on the new building foundation to begin, I also tried to sort through the pieces of the murder case strewn about in my head. Neil had been less than helpful when I visited him the previous weekend, and I felt as if I had been rehashing the same details over and over without making any progress. There had to be something that everyone, including myself, had missed.

As we cleared the last of the debris, Hank walked over to us.

"Nice job guys. You made short work of that."

"Thanks," Jeff answered. "It always goes more quickly working together."

I paused as he said it. It was a simple expression and had Jeff said it at any other time I wouldn't have thought twice about it. But since I had been thinking about Neil and the case all morning, it prompted something in my mind that could be important. What if someone else had been involved with Evelyn's murder? Even if it hadn't been planned and Neil acted alone in killing her, maybe he had help getting rid of the body.

As soon as work was over, I drove directly to Charles Vaughn's home. He seemed surprised to see me, but quickly invited me in.

"I'm just putting some dinner on the table," he said. "Would you like to join me?"

"No thanks. I don't want to put you out at all. I just needed to ask you a few more questions."

"It's no bother at all...I made plenty. Have a seat," he said, motioning me towards the small table in his kitchen.

After a quick description of my trip to see Neil the previous weekend, I told him about my recent thoughts regarding the case and asked if he thought Neil might have had help from someone else.

"It's an interesting theory." Charles answered. "To be honest, if there was one thing that always bothered me about the case it was the timing of the events the night of Evelyn's murder."

"What do you mean?"

"It would have taken quite a bit of time for Neil to not only kill Evelyn, but to remove her body from the park, dispose of it, and then bury her clothes somewhere else. And since he disappeared so quickly afterwards and was able to evade everyone that was out looking for him, it could support your idea that he had some help."

Charles and I discussed the possible timing of the events of the night of August 23, 1965. Evelyn left her home around 10:45 PM, and had been seen at the park between 11:00 PM and 11:15 PM. Since the crime scene wasn't discovered at the Gold Nugget until after 2:00 AM, that left about a three-hour window when Evelyn could have been murdered. Even if she had been killed as early as 12:00 AM, Neil probably wouldn't have been able to remove her body from the park until at least 1:00 in the morning. Although Evelyn was a petite girl, carrying that much dead weight would still be difficult for him to do by himself, and by that time they had already been searching the grounds for her for at least an hour or more. So, how did Neil get her body out without being seen? And once he did, there was no sign of him at all around the local area after 4:00 AM when the police began looking for him.

"So, you think someone else could have been involved?" I asked.

"Of course, but I'm not sure who would have helped him. He had burned a lot of bridges over the years, so to speak, and I can't think of anyone that would have been willing to stick their neck out for him."

I picked at the tuna casserole on my plate.

"What about his father?" I asked.

"Well, I guess that's possible. His father had a long rap sheet and had been in a fair amount of trouble over the years. But he left the Hershey area when Neil was seventeen and as far as we knew hadn't returned or had any contact with Neil."

"What about his co-workers at Hershey Park? Do you think any of them might have been involved?"

"I doubt it. Joe Peterson never would have helped him. In fact, there's probably nothing he would have liked better than to see Neil locked up."

"Could there have been someone else there who would have been in a position to help him? Was anyone else at the park the night of the murder?"

Charles smiled. "You're starting to sound like a detective."

"I don't know about that," I told him. "I'm just trying to figure this whole thing out."

"From what I learned during my investigation there were only three other people scheduled to be there that night: two maintenance workers and the head of security."

"Who was in charge of security?" I asked.

"Richard Barr was his name. He was the first person on the scene and the one who called it in. He was also the last person to see Evelyn alive."

"So, he would have been in a position to help Neil kill her, or at least help him get rid of her body."

"Sure, but I don't know why he would have. We questioned him extensively in the days following the murder and didn't find any reason to think he was involved. He was also set to retire in a few weeks, and had no motive. Besides, after Neil confessed he could have easily implicated Richard or anyone else, but didn't."

"But there has to be a reason Neil has kept quiet about so many things," I said. "Protecting someone else seems like the only possible explanation."

CHAPTER 16

August 23, 1965

Evelyn could feel her heart pounding in her chest as she raced across the grounds of the empty amusement park. She couldn't see him anywhere, but somehow knew he was close by. She could sense it. After months of seeing Neil, it had finally come to this. But there was no turning back now, and the past could not be changed. If she could only reach the Gold Nugget, she knew she would be safe and everything would be fine. As she passed the Carousel, she stumbled and landed flat on the pavement, scraping her hands and tearing the knee of her pants. Ignoring the pain, she picked herself up and continued on, glancing behind her as she ran.

July 29, 1978

I turned the key to my VW and listened to the low growl of the exhaust. The sun was slowly rising on another Saturday morning and the sky was clear. The day before, Pete Rose had extended his hitting streak to forty-one games, managing to reach base in both games of a double header against the Phillies. For the first time in thirty-seven years, it appeared that Joe Dimaggio's seemingly untouchable record might finally be broken. I had been trying my best to catch the recent games on television as the hard-charging Cincinnati Red inched closer to the mark, but since my visit to Graterford prison the previous weekend I had little time to think about anything but work. The construction of the new building for the Fender Bender had gotten off to a slow start and, along with several other projects at Hershey Park, it was now behind schedule. Mr. Hall had put us on mandatory overtime until things were back on track. We were working twelve-hour days that week and although I appreciated the extra money, I was glad for a day off.

When I needed to clear my head I would often get in my car and drive aimlessly, and that was my plan for the day. I adjusted the tuning knob on my stereo until F&M's

college radio station came in clearly, and settled in for the drive. A few turns on the local roads north of town took me to Route 81. As I pulled onto the highway, Bram Tchaikovsky's *Girl of My Dreams* played. My thoughts went immediately to Jess and, before long, to Evelyn Welsh.

As far as Evelyn was concerned, I felt like I had reached a dead end. The realization that Jeff and I had about Neil wanting her belongings to be found seemed like it could be significant, but why? It also seemed likely that someone else was involved, and that Neil's silence was intended to protect them. Only Neil knew the answers, and he clearly wasn't going to tell me anything more. Besides, I had found little else to go on, and was starting to think I should just let all of this go. Maybe the best way to honor Evelyn's memory was to just let her rest in peace, wherever she was.

I thought about her family, and wondered how they had managed to go on with so many questions remaining unanswered about their daughter. I heard that her parents had moved away from town the year following Evelyn's murder. It must have been hard for them to remain there and be constantly reminded of her, so it wasn't surprising to me they made the decision to move on. Several years later, they both died in a terrible car accident, so at least there was some solace in knowing they were finally reunited with their daughter.

I also thought about Neil and his sister, and how it must have been difficult for her to come to terms with what he had done. We're always the hardest on the people we care about, but when it comes down to it, are also the first ones to defend them. I wondered what the conversations between them had been like when she visited him in prison.

I've always believed that our minds are incredibly powerful, and are often working subconsciously on problems even when we're not aware of it. As I thought about Neil's sister, it occurred to me that maybe she was the one person that Neil had trusted enough to tell things he wouldn't tell anyone else. Even if Neil wouldn't talk, maybe his sister could be convinced to talk…especially if their relationship had deteriorated over the years. After all, the woman at the prison did say her visits had dropped off and then stopped. Maybe it was the break I had been looking for.

With a new sense of hope I took the next exit ramp off the highway and looked for a gas station. I found one just off the exit, pulled in, and searched frantically through my car for some spare change for the pay phone. I was about to give up when I found a lone quarter hidden between the floor mat and the carpet.

I still had Charles Vaughn's phone number in my wallet, and dialed it quickly. Fortunately, I caught him at home. I apologized for bothering him again, and asked what he knew about Neil's sister and if he had any idea how I could get in contact with her.

"I'm sorry, but what are you talking about?" he asked, sounding confused.

"What do you mean, what am I talking about?"

He paused before answering.

"Neil doesn't have a sister."

CHAPTER 17

August 23, 1965

After what seemed to be an eternity, she reached the Gold Nugget and ducked in through the unlocked side door. Neil, who had been gaining ground on her, reached the door shortly after her. As he burst through the doorway, Evelyn gasped and turned to him.

"Why are you doing this Neil?"

He looked at her and seemed to be searching for the right words.

"Because it's the right thing to do. And I've never done the right thing in my life."

"You know they're going to think you did it."

"Don't worry about that. Everything will be fine."

Neil went to the corner and grabbed the plastic drum he had hidden earlier. It was fortunate that he and Evelyn had the same blood type. It had saved a lot of time collecting enough to make the whole thing convincing, he thought as he poured the blood onto the floor, being careful not to step in it. Besides, the needle marks on their arms from drawing blood were getting more evident as the weeks passed, and he knew that Evelyn's friends and others close to her were beginning to have concerns about what she was doing when they were together. Not a single person would be concerned about the marks on his arms though. Nobody cared about him, and they never would.

"Okay, are you ready?" he asked Evelyn.

"I think so."

"All right, lean back into my arms and go limp."

She obeyed, and Neil dragged her so her feet slid through the pool of blood, leaving two trails towards the doorway. Then, he lifted her carefully and carried her out the side door of the Gold Nugget. When they were outside and hidden by the shadow of the building, he set her down and she removed her shoes and placed them in a plastic bag. Neil quickly reentered the room and grabbed the drum, and now that he was out of sight of Evelyn stepped in the blood and carefully left enough footprints so they could be identified as his. He took one last look around, and exited again through the side door. Once outside, he removed his shoes as well and placed them in a second bag.

"Okay, let's get down to the creek. I have everything else ready."

Evelyn and Neil picked their way down the steep bank towards Spring Creek. At the bottom of the slope, he made his way into the brush and slid out the old canoe. While making their plans he had questioned whether this part was absolutely necessary, but they couldn't take any chances being seen as they left the park. Especially with Evelyn still alive.

Evelyn crouched low in the canoe while Neil pushed off from the bank and paddled silently in the darkness. Stone walls lined both banks of the creek in that area, and Neil stuck close to one side trying to stay concealed. Spring Creek meandered through the park, and eventually passed under a foot bridge and service road before leaving the park grounds. It was this foot bridge that Evelyn had previously stood on each morning, and it occurred to her that she was not unlike one of the many leaves she had tossed in the creek earlier that summer. She was no longer in control and unsure of what the future held.

The next bridge they would come to was at North Hockersville Road, a little-used road accessing the local sewage treatment plant. It was here that Neil had hidden his car and the few belongings they would need to get away. The two climbed out onto the stream bank, and after retrieving the plastic drum and bag, Neil gave the canoe a shove so it would continue down the creek. Evelyn climbed into the front seat of his car, quickly changed out of the clothes she was wearing, and gave them to Neil. He put them in the plastic bag with her shoes and placed it in the trunk of his car.

Neil waited until they were on the main road to turn on his lights, then drove west towards Falmouth. Before they were halfway there, he pulled off the road into a small gravel parking lot and turned off the engine.

"Is this the place we talked about?" asked Evelyn.

"Yeah," said Neil, "This will only take a little while, but you'd better come along with me. If anyone would happen to stop here, we can't risk having them see you in the car."

He grabbed the bag with Evelyn's shoes and clothes, and stooped down alongside the car. After pulling the clothes out of the bag and rubbing them in the dirt, he doused them with what was left of the blood. Then he grabbed a flashlight and shovel from the trunk and they headed up a dirt trail into the woods.

Half an hour later they were back. As Neil slid back into the driver's seat, a sheet of paper fell silently from the car onto the gravel. The interior dome light provided enough illumination for him to see it was a receipt bearing his name, and he reached down to pick it up. As he did so he hesitated, and after looking over at Evelyn to see if she had noticed, decided to leave it where it fell.

Neil carefully pulled onto Roundtop Road and continued west. After several miles he made another quick stop behind a closed service station, tossed the second bag containing his work boots into a dumpster, then turned north towards U.S. Route 15. It was now after 1:30 AM, and by daybreak they would be out of Pennsylvania. Neil rested his arm on the seat back as he drove, and Evelyn slid closer to him and leaned her head against his chest. Van Morrison's *It's All Over Now* played softly on the car's AM radio, and as she listened to the words Evelyn sighed and closed her eyes. Neil leaned over and kissed her forehead as she drifted off to sleep.

August 1, 1978

After my conversation with Charles Vaughn on the gas station pay phone, I felt like I was closer than ever to figuring out what it was about Evelyn's death and Neil's role in it that had been nagging at me for so long. There was something about it that just hadn't added up, but I couldn't quite put my finger on it. And if Neil didn't have a sister, who had been coming to visit him in prison all those years?

I slumped onto the couch and noticed my copy of *A Tale of Two Cities* sitting on the coffee table. With everything else that had been going on I had been struggling to find the time to read it, but finally finished it earlier that week. It was interesting that Lucie Manette's character had the same blonde hair as Evelyn, and that her father, wrongfully imprisoned for so long in the Bastille, had kept a few strands of it as a reminder of her. From everything I had learned about Evelyn, I felt she was the kind of person that would inspire that kind of devotion from someone who loved her.

I also admired the character of Sydney Carton. At the beginning of the novel he had been looked down on as an alcoholic and anything but a hero, but he ultimately proved otherwise because of his love for Lucie. By selflessly offering himself to be executed in place of her husband Darnay, he fulfilled the promise he had made to her to *"embrace any sacrifice for you and for those dear to you"*.

I thought more about the book's themes of devotion, sacrifice, and redemption and felt there might be an answer hidden somewhere in those pages to the questions that had been troubling me about Evelyn. I picked up the novel and opened it to the beginning of Book One, which was also titled *Recalled to Life*. As I looked at the words, I felt a shiver run through my body and read them again.

Recalled to Life.

And then, things began to fall into place. Was it possible that Evelyn wasn't really dead? Could it have been her that had been coming to see Neil? Deep down I had always wanted to believe that she might still be alive. In fact, that may have been why I kept feeling that her body would never be found. But even if that was the case, why would Neil spend all those years in prison for a crime he didn't commit, and why would Evelyn allow him to do it?

In my mind I searched back through everything I had learned about the case. Nothing in particular jumped out at me until I recalled the first conversation I had with the former detective earlier that summer. It was then that I remembered Charles saying:

"We had a number of different leads we were following up. In a case like this there's no shortage of people calling in with their ideas, and we need to look into them no matter how ridiculous they sound. One guy even suggested that John Welsh had ties to organized crime, and that we should consider the possibility that Evelyn's death may have been a professional hit."

I turned this over in my head. What if her father really was linked to something illegal? What if she felt her life was in danger because of it? Was it possible that she and

Neil staged the whole thing to protect her? I thought about all the planning it would take to pull something like that off, and wondered how two teenagers could have managed it and then kept it quiet for so many years. There's no question that Neil was very smart; it had come up several times during the interviews after Evelyn's supposed murder. It also would have been much easier to disappear and start a new life in 1965 than it would be now. But what could possibly have happened that made her feel she was in such grave danger?

CHAPTER 18

June 22, 1965

Evelyn removed the warm clothes from the dryer and placed them in the laundry basket. It was an unusually slow day at the park, even for a weekday, and she had been sent home early. Since her mother would be gone until later that evening, Evelyn decided to be helpful and do the laundry. Besides, she liked the smell of freshly washed clothes, and she breathed in deeply as she set the basket on top of the dryer.

The laundry room was just off her father's study, separated by a louvered bi-fold door. As she stood there quietly, she could hear footsteps enter the study through the opposite door and then two voices speaking in hushed tones. One was her father's, and the other belonged to Stan Caprizza, one of his business associates.

"Are you sure we're alone?" asked Stan.

"Yeah. Doris has been at her mother's place for a few days, and Evelyn is working. She won't be home for a few more hours."

"Good. Now why are you so upset about up this?"

"Because this isn't what we talked about. I can't believe you did this."

Evelyn had never cared much for Stan. Her unusual ability to read people had raised red flags the few times she had come in contact with him, and as she listened to the conversation she realized the reservations she had about him were justified. She edged closer to the door and could hear Stan's reply.

"John, you and I both agreed that we needed to put some pressure on him. If he continued to underbid you on every single contract, your business would be in even deeper trouble than it already is. Mr. Allen has floated a lot of loans to keep you solvent, and this was in the best interest of everyone."

"But you were just supposed to rough him up...send him a message. You weren't supposed to kill him!" countered John.

"Hey, things happen. We offered to buy him out, very generously I might add, and he kept refusing. He had his chance to walk away from this."

"But what will Mr. Allen say when he finds out? He doesn't like anyone making this kind of move without him giving the okay."

"He's not going to find out. I made it look like an accident...a very fortunate one for all of us, but an accident nonetheless. And you won't tell him either. This is going to stay between the two of us."

Evelyn couldn't believe what she was hearing. She knew her father's business had been struggling and that Stan had recently offered to help him, but she never imagined it involved anything like this. She could feel herself shaking and knew she had to leave before her father and Stan realized she had overheard them. But as she backed slowly away from the door, her sleeve caught on a dust mop propped in the corner. Before she could catch it, the mop hit a container of laundry detergent sitting on the edge of the washer, and both crashed loudly to the floor. Her heart sank.

She heard Stan's footsteps move quickly across the study, and the bi-fold door swung open violently. Evelyn gasped as he stared at her with a look of hatred burning in his eyes.

<u>August 2, 1978</u>

I dialed the number for the State Correctional Institution at Graterford and asked for the visitation desk. I remembered that Sandy was the name of woman at the desk the day I visited, and asked if she was available. She wasn't, and the man who did answer didn't seem to be in any hurry to help. I asked if he could check the sign-in sheets for the name of Neil Fischer's sister, but apparently they only kept the sheets for a month and then they were filed away in the records room. Besides, they weren't permitted to give out any information about visitors. Even though the residents there were convicted criminals, they still had a right to certain amount of privacy. I thanked him anyway, and left my name and number and a message asking Sandy to give me a call back.

When she finally returned my call, she confirmed that she shouldn't have mentioned Neil's sister the day I was there, and really couldn't help me any further. She was sympathetic, however, and seemed like she wanted to help.

I listened as she explained, "You know, if it was an official request, like from an attorney or a law enforcement officer, the information could be made available. Do you know anyone like that?"

It just so happened I did know a law enforcement officer… a retired one anyway.

Later that day as I sat in Detective Vaughn's den, I listened to his half of the conversation with the records room clerk at Graterford. Charles left out the fact that he was now retired, but explained that he had been the investigating detective on the case and that there were some new leads regarding the location of Evelyn Welsh's remains. It was important that he question anyone that may have had contact with Neil in prison, especially any family members.

After being told he would need to fill out the appropriate forms and either mail them or drop them off in person, he said, "I understand that's your policy, but we really need to act on this quickly."

A terse reply came from the other end of the line, which Charles answered in a raised voice, "Do you really want me to tell this girl's family that your ill-conceived bureaucratic policies kept us from finding her in a timely manner?"

Another answer followed, which Charles interrupted.

"Don't you think Evelyn's family has waited long enough?"

After a somewhat longer response on the other end, his voice softened.

"Thank you. I appreciate it very much. Yes, I can hold for a few minutes."

In a short amount of time the clerk returned with a name.

CHAPTER 19

<u>August 31, 1965:</u>

The motel room clock showed 6:05 AM as Neil put on his shoes and a light jacket. He placed a folded note on the nightstand by Evelyn's bed, and stood there for a minute watching her as she slept. A few tresses of her once blonde hair fell over her face. It was now dyed a dark brown, but she looked every bit as beautiful as the day he first saw her. He kissed her cheek before slipping out of the room, knowing it would be the last time he did so, and drove several miles away to a small roadside diner. The hat and sunglasses he had worn the past week to make sure he wasn't recognized still lay on a small table in the motel room.

As he opened the front door of the diner, Neil could smell fresh coffee brewing and bacon frying. He stood by the cigarette machine at the entrance, looking around casually. After putting the correct change into the machine, he pulled the lever and lifted the door to grab a pack of Camels. As he smacked it against his palm to pack the tobacco, he looked at the stack of newspapers for sale. Just as he had expected, his picture was displayed prominently on the front page along with a lengthy story about the ongoing search for Evelyn. He bought a copy, took a seat at the counter, and set the paper down next to him. A waitress walked over and offered him coffee.

"Yes, ma'am. Black."

She filled his mug and placed a menu in front of him. A few minutes later she was back to take his order.

"What'll it be, brown eyes?"

"Two eggs over light, bacon, and toast."

"Coming right up," she replied as she scribbled on her pad.

The waitress placed his order on the carousel and rang the bell. While he waited for his breakfast, Neil read the news article about Evelyn's apparent murder and the ongoing hunt for him. The clothes he planted in the woods had been discovered the previous Saturday, which meant it had taken the authorities more than four days to find them. It made no mention of the blood-covered work boots he had discarded in the service station dumpster just south of Middletown. He shook his head in disgust. Maybe he had overestimated their ability to find the evidence he so carefully left. He was relieved, at least, that he had decided not to pick up the receipt he dropped in the State Game Lands parking lot. Without it, they may not have found Evelyn's clothes at all. Still, he wondered if that would be enough to lead their search in the direction of the river.

The waitress returned with his food and he set the paper aside. Neil ate slowly, savoring each bite, like a death row inmate consuming his last meal. As he finished the last slice of bacon and took another sip of coffee, he sighed quietly to himself. He wondered how long it would be, if ever, until he would have another decent meal.

Seeing his cup was almost empty, the waitress returned with a pot of coffee. As she topped it off, she glanced down at the newspaper laying on the counter beside him. Neil had folded it so his picture was clearly visible, and he watched as her eyes moved from his face, to the photograph, and back again. The coffee she was pouring ran over the sides of his cup and spilled across the counter.

"Oh no! I'm so sorry," she said nervously.

The waitress quickly cleaned up the mess and hurried into the kitchen. Neil could hear hushed conversation coming from the back, and before long a man who appeared to be the owner emerged from the kitchen and walked across the diner to a table at the far side of the room. He stood with his back to Neil, conversing with a man with a crew cut sitting at the table. Neil could see the owner motioning with his head towards his side of the room, and before long the man with the crew cut stood up and slowly made his way over to him. As he approached, Neil could see his hand was resting on a revolver tucked in his waist band.

"Excuse me," the man said cautiously, "but I'm going to need to ask you to step outside with me for a minute."

"I thought you might," replied Neil as he slowly got up from his stool and walked out of the diner with his hands at his side.

He could already hear sirens in the distance.

<u>August 5, 1978</u>

The name we had been given by the records clerk at Graterford was Stacy Gordon. We knew that Ms. Gordon, if that's who she really was, most likely lived within a day or two driving time of the prison. Any further than that and it would have been difficult to visit as frequently as she had. That still left a pretty large radius, but as Detective Vaughn and I discussed it we came to the conclusion we should begin with the area of New York where Neil had been arrested. If the whole thing had really been staged to help Evelyn disappear, Neil probably would have stuck close to her until she reached wherever it was she was going.

Charles still had a number of friends in the department willing to provide him with access to information. Ben Harnish, one of his old colleagues, agreed to help and within a short amount of time we had a list of all the Stacy Gordons living in upstate New York. There were four. The first two we eliminated pretty quickly. Stacy L. Gordon was a 77-year old retired school teacher who had lived in the Tupper Lake area all her life, and Stacy M. Gordon was a 12-year old junior high student in Utica. That left two Stacy E. Gordons, one a 29-year old unmarried woman from Harrisville and the other a 31-year old mother of two in Rome, New York.

Rome was the larger of the two towns and also the closest, so Charles and I decided to start there. When I arrived at his house that morning, I found him waiting in his car, ready to go. Even in retirement he had kept up his old habit of rising before dawn each morning. Four and a half hours later, as we passed the Fort Stanwix National Monument on our way into town, I looked forward in anticipation to what we might find.

The address Ben had given us was on North Madison Street near the center of town, and as we approached the Victorian-style two-story home we could see a woman tending to a flower bed in the shade of the front yard. Charles slowed down so we could get a closer look without stopping. She was bending over, facing away from us, but I could tell she was thin and similar in height to Evelyn. She stood up as we passed, and my pulse quickened when I saw the shoulder-length blonde hair that had fallen over her face as she worked.

I turned to Charles and asked, "So, what are we going to say to her?"

"The best thing to do is to just stop and act like we need directions," he answered. "That will give us a reason to talk to her without raising any suspicions. If we're not sure if it's her right away, we can always start a longer conversation. You know, talk about the weather... anything at all."

"Got it. And what if it is her?" I asked.

Until that moment I hadn't even considered what we would do if we actually found Evelyn.

"Let's not worry about that just yet. This is long shot, so don't be disappointed if we don't find her."

Charles pulled into an on-street parking spot just past the house, and as we climbed out of the car I grabbed the

New York state map from the glove box. As we approached her I opened it to the Rome inset to lend some credibility to our act.

"Good morning ma'am," called out Charles. "It's a nice day, isn't it?"

"It sure is," she answered pleasantly as she brushed back her sun-streaked hair and pushed it behind her ear.

"I'm really sorry to bother you, but we seem to be lost."

"Where are you heading?"

As Charles talked to the woman, I looked her over closely. Her skin was darkly tanned and she wore a faded navy-blue polo shirt and white tennis skirt. A small monogram on her shirt sleeve contained the initials S.E.G., confirming she was the Stacey Gordon we were looking for. She had the right build and hair color, but I couldn't have said for sure whether it was Evelyn.

"We're trying to find the Capitol Theatre," answered Charles. "I thought it was around here somewhere, but I don't have the street address."

"Oh, that's interesting. I hope you're not planning to see any recent movies there. They've run into some difficult times the past few years and have only been showing second-run films."

"Actually, I'm not much of a movie buff...I'd rather

read a good book. But I am a fan of the art deco movement, and I've heard the theatre is a pretty good example."

"Well, in that case you're in luck. It's just a few blocks back on West Dominick."

I could see why Charles had been such an accomplished detective. He had done his research and was prepared to engage her for as long as we needed. Meanwhile, I continued to watch every movement of her face as they talked.

"Thank you, ma'am. Is it close enough to walk to, or should we drive?"

"Well, parking can be a problem on that street, so you might want to walk. Besides, it's a beautiful day," she answered.

As she spoke, she stepped out of the shade into the sunlight, and I looked more closely at her eyes. People can age, gain or lose weight, and change their hair color or style. But their eye color doesn't change, and this woman's eyes were hazel, not blue. My heart sank as I realized it wasn't Evelyn.

Charles must have reached the same conclusion, because shortly afterwards he thanked her again for the directions and wished her a nice day. Ms. Gordon must have sensed our disappointment, and as we turned and walked back to the car she called out after us.

"Something tells me you're not really looking for the Capitol Theatre, are you?"

Charles and I looked at each other, then back at her.

"No, we're not," I answered.

"Well, whatever it is, or whoever it is you're looking for, I hope you find them."

"Thanks ma'am," said Charles. "I'm sorry for bothering you."

"It's quite alright."

I was frustrated, but as we left Rome, Charles explained that detective work usually involves a lot of effort with few results. It was a process of eliminating possibilities more than anything else, and that was exactly what we had done.

We stopped for burgers and fries at a local restaurant before driving the remaining two hours to Harrisville. The rest of the ride was spent in silence as we passed the small towns and farms nestled in the foothills of the Adirondacks. It was late in the day when we finally approached Harrisville, and Charles decided we should get a cheap motel room on the outskirts of town and start fresh in the morning. It was fine with me since I had experienced enough disappointment for one day.

CHAPTER 20

August 6, 1978

Harrisville was a quiet community of about nine hundred people located in Lewis County, New York. The West Branch of the Oswegatchie River bisected the town on its way from the Adirondack Mountains to the Saint Lawrence River, and as the former detective and I drove through town early that Sunday morning, the pace seemed as slow as the river itself during the dry months of summer.

Charles pulled his Ford LTD off the road a few properties away from a small wood frame house on Church Street, about halfway between Pilgrim Holiness Church and River Street. He was careful not to park directly in front of it. The previous day had been frustrating, and part of me was beginning to think this may just be another waste of time. I had no good reason, other than a hunch, to believe that the Stacy who had been visiting Neil was actually Evelyn, and I questioned what we were even doing there as we approached the front door and rang the bell. There was no answer.

Charles lit his pipe and leaned against the car as we decided on our next move. The August sun was already warming the air, and we could hear singing coming from the church a short distance down the street.

"Maybe we should have called first. She may not even be around," I suggested.

"You might be right. But if it is Evelyn, we couldn't take the chance of tipping her off that we were coming to see her. If she's been hiding for thirteen years you can bet there's a good reason she doesn't want to be found."

I nodded and glanced up the street.

"Maybe she's at church."

Charles looked at me, shrugged, and put out his pipe. "I haven't set foot inside a church in years."

"Let's take a look."

It was a small congregation, and about forty people were scattered throughout the pews. We entered quietly and slid into the last row as inconspicuously as possible. We were slightly underdressed for the occasion, but the atmosphere in the church seemed inviting and no one appeared to be bothered by our presence. Several members near the back nodded to us as we took our seats.

I looked around the room as the opening hymns continued. It was much different than the type of service I was accustomed to. My parents were devout Catholics and from a young age I obediently attended Mass with them, took the sacrament of First Communion, and went through Confirmation. Now that I was living away from home, I even tried to make it to an occasional service at the Sacred Heart Parish near F&M's campus. However, I still had moments where I questioned what I believed and whether it was genuinely my own faith or if I was just doing what had always been expected of me.

I wasn't the first person my age to experience these doubts, and certainly wouldn't be the last. And although I wasn't yet at the point where I had all the answers, there was one thing I did know for sure. Both good and evil existed around us, and the difference was so marked I knew there had to be a basis for morality beyond each of us deciding for ourselves what was right or wrong. Acting in one's own self-interest was one thing, but the unspeakable acts of cruelty that had occurred throughout history left no doubt in my mind there were dark forces at work in this world. And conversely, I knew the selfless acts of compassion and sacrifice I had seen were not just random, uninspired actions. It was this that I held to firmly even as I questioned everything else.

My thoughts were interrupted as the hymns ended and the minister began his sermon with a scripture reading.

"The fifteenth chapter of the book of John tells us this: 'Greater love hath no man than this, that a man lay down his life for his friends.'" He continued, "Almost two thousand years ago, someone did exactly that for you and me. It was the embodiment of every parable He told and every directive He ever gave about loving your neighbor as yourself. And so, this verse is also a command telling what is expected of us as believers. If Christ was willing to lay down his life for each person sitting here today who didn't deserve it, we need to ask ourselves whether we are willing to do the same for others."

His message was compelling, but it was difficult to pay attention as I looked over the people seated in front of me. Most of the congregation was older, but one woman in the third row looked to be in her late twenties or early thirties. She sat alone, and I kept watching her hoping she might turn to the side so I could get a better look at her. Unfortunately, she never did, and when the service ended she stood up and exited through a side door towards the front of the sanctuary. Charles had noticed her as well, and we looked at each other and left through the main door where we had entered.

We stood at the corner of the church, partially hidden by a large azalea bush. From there we could see her walking up Church Street towards our parked car. As she passed it, she glanced at the Pennsylvania plates, pausing briefly in her tracks, and continued on to the house we had visited earlier.

"That must be her," I said, "Let's go."

We followed at a safe distance until she entered the home, then climbed the porch steps for a second time and rang the bell. No answer. After another ring we heard footsteps inside, and the door swung open slowly.

"Can I help you?" asked the woman at the door.

I wanted to answer, but couldn't speak. I knew immediately the woman standing in the doorway was Evelyn. Her hair was brown and much longer than it had been years ago. There were also small wrinkles at the corners of her eyes and a few worry lines across her forehead, but there was no doubt in my mind it was the same person in the pictures I had seen so many times. Her eyes confirmed it. They were as blue as a cloudless summer sky and there was no mistaking them.

Detective Vaughn was the first to speak, "Stacy Gordon?"

"Uh, yes. Do I know you?" she replied.

"No ma'am, you don't." He pulled his identification from his pocket and showed it to her. "My name is Charles Vaughn and I'm a former detective from the Hershey, Pennsylvania area. I was wondering if we could ask you a few questions."

At the mention of his name, the color left her face. It occurred to me that she would have followed the news about the investigation of her murder and probably recognized his name from years earlier.

She hesitated, then said reluctantly, "Please come in."

"Thank you, Stacy. Or would you prefer Evelyn?"

CHAPTER 21

August 6, 1978

We sat in Evelyn's living room as she recounted the events that led up to the early morning hours of August 24, 1965. The child-like innocence so prevalent in those early photos was now gone from her face. She was no longer a girl, but a woman whose beauty had been tempered by the hardships and disappointments of life.

She told us about the day in her father's study when Stan Caprizza caught her listening in on their conversation, and how he had threatened to kill her and her parents if she ever mentioned it to anyone. Her father wasn't concerned about his own life; he knew he had made a mistake and was willing to pay whatever price that required. But he was distraught afterwards thinking that Stan might follow through on his threat to kill Evelyn, even if she never talked. Stan had too much to lose and

John Welsh knew that his daughter would never be safe.

"But why didn't you just go to the police and tell them what happened?" I asked. "It all could have ended right there."

Evelyn continued, "We would have, but Stan had someone inside the police force, a corrupt cop he had bribed over the years to avoid investigations into his business practices. My father had no idea who it was and couldn't take any chances going to them. Even if he went higher up to the State Police or the FBI, he couldn't be sure they would figure out who was involved before it was too late."

"So you decided to fake your own death," I said.

"It was Neil's idea. My parents only went along with it because they felt they had no other choice."

I recalled the articles I had read where Evelyn's parents had been interviewed soon after her disappearance. Her parents had seemed so distraught, especially Doris, and it was all very convincing. Her mother's acting experience had served her well.

"But from everything I read there was so much blood at the scene," I questioned, "How could anyone fake that?"

"We knew that without a body there would need to be compelling evidence I had actually died. It seemed simple enough that if a lot of blood was found at the scene, more than someone could possibly lose and still survive without medical attention, it would be more convincing. If Neil and I didn't have the same blood type I don't think we could have pulled it off. Neil was sure they would type the blood, of course, and we were already pushing the limit on how much I could draw myself. Everything Neil had read said the recovery time after giving blood was at least twenty days, even up to sixty days in some cases. We each did it several times over a six-week period, and each time we drew more than we probably should have. We wanted to make sure we had enough, and it completely drained us. Our arms were also getting badly bruised from the needles…we weren't exactly experts at drawing blood. Then there was the problem of keeping it until we needed it. Neil knew there needed to be enough red blood cells still surviving for it to appear fresh and to be typed. So in addition to gathering a lot of it in a short amount of time, we had to keep it in the refrigerator in his apartment until we were ready to use it."

Detective Vaughn interrupted. "But with Neil planning to confess, why did you need to go to all that trouble?"

Evelyn looked at him and tears began to well up in her eyes.

"Because I didn't know he was going to confess. I didn't even know he was planning all along to get caught. But he knew the authorities would keep looking for him, and me too unless everyone was convinced I was dead. So, he allowed himself to be captured and confessed to the murder."

Evelyn left the room and returned with a piece of paper, worn by the years. "He left me this note the morning he snuck out of our motel room and went to the diner."

Charles unfolded it and read it. When he was finished he handed it to me.

Dear Evelyn,

By the time you read this, I'll probably be in police custody. I'm sorry I wasn't honest with you about what I was planning to do, but I didn't want you to try to stop me. I'm going to tell them I did it, because you'll never be safe unless I do. You'll be fine as long as you stick to the rest of our plan.

Promise me you'll never tell anyone the truth. I haven't led a very good life, but saving you will be the one good thing I've ever done. Please don't take that away from me.

-Neil

I folded the note and gave it back to Evelyn.

"It's torn me apart knowing that Neil has suffered for me all these years," she said. "You don't know how many times I've thought about telling someone, but I guess I don't have a choice now."

"Not necessarily," replied Charles, "At least not right away."

Evelyn and I both looked at him.

He continued, "I need some time to figure out what to do. First, I need to look into this Stan Caprizza and see if there's enough to build a case against him. But it's going to be tricky. If there was somebody corrupt on the force, they may still be there, and poking around might just tip them off that something's going on. It's been thirteen years, but you can bet there are still people that will have a lot to lose if this breaks open. Who knows, it may even go higher up than we think."

"Okay," agreed Evelyn, looking directly at Charles, then at me. "I don't have any other choice but to trust you."

I tried to put myself in her position, having to rely on two complete strangers to maintain the secret she and Neil had kept for so long.

Shortly afterward, we said our goodbyes to Evelyn.

She begged us to be careful, and after agreeing that we would, Charles and I got into his LTD and headed back to Pennsylvania. Most of the long drive home was spent discussing how we should best proceed and the importance of keeping Evelyn safe. It was late Sunday night when we finally pulled into the driveway at Detective Vaughn's house, and I was exhausted. All I wanted to do at that point was get back to my room and get some sleep.

As I walked to my car, I noticed a large late-model sedan parked on the street two houses away. There were no street lamps and in the darkness it was difficult to see, but I was pretty sure I could make out someone sitting in the driver's seat. I glanced in the rear-view mirror as I started my car, and as I drove away the sedan's headlights turned on. It seemed to be tailing me at a distance for three blocks, and as I made a left turn at the next street it continued to follow me. I decided to circle back to see if it was intentional or just a coincidence, but as I made the next left, the sedan turned right and disappeared down a side street.

You're just being paranoid, I told myself.

CHAPTER 22

August 7, 1978:

It was three in the morning when I finally collapsed onto my bed after our trip back from New York. Despite being exhausted, there was so much running through my head I barely slept the rest of the night. I tossed and turned for hours, and when I finally did drift off it seemed like only minutes had passed when my 6:30 AM alarm was rudely waking me.

I knew it was going to be a rough morning, so I stopped at a convenience store for a large coffee on my way to work. I put the exact change down on the counter and thanked the attendant. As she slid the coins off the counter I noticed a Special Olympics donation cannister sitting nearby, and it made me think of Joey and Jess.

It was only then I remembered I had promised to call

her the day before. My heart sank. We had been trading phone calls the past week, missing each other each time, and the last message I left with her mother was that I would definitely call her Sunday evening. In the excitement of figuring out Evelyn might still be alive, and then actually finding her, I had completely forgotten about Jess. I felt terrible. At the risk of being late for work, I walked over to the pay phone outside and dialed her number. There was no answer. At that point I could do nothing more but get back into my car.

Somehow, I made it through the morning, and when lunch time came I sat down with Jeff. I made sure we were far enough away from the other workers so I could fill him in on what had happened.

"So, what's on your mind?" he asked. "You've been distracted all morning. And you look terrible, by the way."

I lowered my voice and looked around to be sure no one else would be able to hear.

"Evelyn is still alive. Charles and I found her."

His jaw dropped in disbelief.

"You're kidding me!"

Jeff listened with rapt attention as I told him how we had figured out Evelyn was still alive, that Charles and I had found her in Harrisville, and that she could be in danger if anyone else knew. He swore he would keep quiet about it, and I knew I could trust him completely.

By mid-afternoon I could barely keep my eyes open and told Mr. Hall I wasn't feeling well. Jeff vouched for me, and his dad was kind enough to let me clock out early. After a long nap back at my apartment I was doing much better. That evening I dialed Jess's number again, and this time she answered.

"Hey Jess, I'm so sorry I didn't call last night. I ended up going out of town and didn't get back until really late."

"That's okay Chad," she said, "I understand."

I could tell by her voice that she didn't really understand.

"I know I've been distracted lately," I told her. "I really wish I could explain why, but I can't."

She sighed and asked, "Is it someone else? You know, if there's another girl you're interested in, you can tell me. We haven't made any promises to each other or anything. And if it's something else, no matter what, you can tell me that too."

Hearing Jess say those words just made it all the more difficult to keep everything from her. I didn't want her to be hurt, but I also knew that I couldn't tell her anything. It was tearing me apart.

"It's another girl, isn't it?" she asked again.

"No, not exactly," I answered, thinking of Evelyn.

"What's her name?"

"I'm sorry. I just can't say any more about it."

"That's okay, I get it. I completely understand, but I really thought you were different. You seemed like someone who knew what he wanted and didn't need to run around with a bunch of different girls to figure that out. But if you're not there yet, that's fine."

I wanted so badly to tell her the truth. I needed to tell her that I really was there, that I did know what I wanted, and that she was what I wanted. But until I could be completely honest with her, I knew it was pointless. So I said nothing.

"Listen Chad, I need to go. I promised Joey I would take him out for ice cream."

Part of me wanted to beg her to stay on the line, but I knew better. I needed to let her go.

"Ok, bye," was all I could say.

"Bye," she said and hung up.

January 18, 1969

Evelyn stood on a hill at the far side of the Hershey Cemetery, her identity hidden by dark glasses and a plaid wool scarf wrapped around her head. She wore a heavy down coat to fend off the winter chill, and held a small bouquet of pink carnations in her hand. Her fur-lined half boots shuffled in the newly fallen snow as she read the inscription on the grave stone in front of her. It belonged to Raymond Hess, born on May 4, 1898, deceased December 12, 1963. Evelyn had no idea who the man was or what he had experienced in his sixty-five years on this earth. She had chosen the grave at random, simply because its location provided a view of the activities taking place on the other side of the cemetery. It was also far enough away that she wouldn't be recognized by anyone attending the funeral service at her family's plot.

Two days earlier Evelyn had picked up a copy of *The Sentinel*, the Dauphin County, Pennsylvania newspaper, as she often did to keep up on events happening in her home town. It was her only real connection to her past besides the brief phone calls with her parents. Even when they did talk, both were careful to drive quite a distance from their homes and use a series of pay phones Neil had scouted out years before. Evelyn's face had gone white as she scanned the local news section and saw the headline: *Hershey Couple Perishes in Single-Car Accident*. The article explained that John and Doris Welsh had been returning home from a long weekend in the Poconos. Investigators at the scene determined they had been heading south as they descended through a mountain pass near Palmerton, and failed to brake around a hairpin turn. There were no witnesses, but according to the accident report their sedan left the highway, flipped over at least twice, and burst into flames. Evelyn felt sick as she read the details, and recalled how much her parents had been looking forward to the weekend away. When they had last talked several weeks earlier, her mother had told her about their plans. Their marriage had been under constant stress the past few years, and she hoped some time alone together would help to heal their struggling relationship.

Evelyn watched as the two caskets were lowered into the ground. Regardless of how things had been for her parents recently, they would now rest together indefinitely. This was the first and only time she had risked returning to her hometown, and as she stood there she could make out the figures of her relatives: aunts, uncles, and cousins she hadn't seen in over four years. The line of mourners filed slowly past the open graves, each one stopping momentarily to drop a flower onto the caskets below or somberly place a shovelful of dirt in the holes.

At first, Evelyn hadn't noticed the man in the long gray overcoat waiting with the others. But as he approached the front of the line, she realized it was Stan Caprizza. Her skin crawled at the sight of him, just as it had each time she had encountered him in the past. As he waited, he looked around the cemetery and for a moment his gaze seemed to settle on her. Evelyn felt herself begin to panic. Her immediate thought was to turn quickly and hurry back to her car, but she knew that would be a mistake. She had questioned whether she should have even come there at all, but to call attention to herself now would be just plain foolish. Instead, she knelt down and placed the carnations at the base of Raymond Hess's gravestone. As she did, she glanced out of the corner of her eye in Stan's direction. He still appeared to be looking directly at her, but as the line moved forward his attention was turned to the shovel being handed to him. She could breathe once again. He hadn't recognized her after all, and gave no other sign he had even noticed her.

CHAPTER 23

August 12, 1978:

Nearly a week had passed since our trip to Harrisville, New York. Since then, Charles and I had agreed to keep our communications to a minimum. There were already a handful of people who might have an idea what we were up to, and we didn't want anyone to start putting the pieces together. Evelyn's life depended on it. He also suggested I compile a list of anyone I may have talked to about my investigations into the case. Fortunately, it was a short list. Because I had been embarrassed about my obsession with Evelyn, Jeff was the only person I had opened up to about it. He was a trusted friend and had already been sworn to secrecy on the matter, so that only left the others. They included the librarian who had helped me with my research, Sandy from the visitation desk at

Graterford, and the prison records clerk. It would be quite a stretch for any of them to figure out what was going on and that Evelyn might still be alive.

Since it was Saturday and all I could do was wait to hear from Charles, I needed to find something to distract me. I made the short trip down the steps to the side door of the Hall's house, and stuck my head in. Jeff's mom was busy with her Saturday afternoon ritual of cleaning the kitchen.

"Hi Mrs. Hall. Is Jeff around?"

"I think he's up in his room. Go on up."

I thanked her and bounded up the stairs. Jeff was laying on his bed engrossed in a dog-eared paperback of *Jaws*.

"I didn't know you read books," I said.

"I don't normally. But this particular edition includes a picture of Chrissie Watkins running down the beach without her clothes on. I've been studying it carefully."

"You're an idiot."

"I know. Mom even threatened to draw a bikini on her with a permanent marker if I didn't stop looking at it."

I just laughed and shook my head. "Do you think you can pull yourself away from Chrissie long enough to get some Chinese food?"

"Sure. Jade Tiki Inn?"

"Of course."

Jeff offered to drive, so we hopped in his truck and headed to the Park City Mall. The Jade Tiki Inn was located in the Gimbels wing of the mall, and was a popular spot for F&M College students. The menu included a mix of Chinese and Polynesian cuisine, considered to be the best in Lancaster.

As we entered the restaurant, we followed our normal routine of rubbing the belly of the Buddha statue for luck before crossing the little wooden bridge into the dining area. Mrs. Ku, the owner's wife, greeted us and showed us to our table.

"How are you boys doing?" she asked.

"Never better, Mrs. Ku," replied Jeff. "What's good today?"

"Everything's good. You know that," she answered as she seated us at a corner table.

Mrs. Ku gave us a few minutes then returned to take our orders. I ordered my usual Szechuan Chicken and a Coke, while Jeff went for the Beef Lo Mein.

"And I'll have a Mai-Tai as well," he added.

Mrs. Ku looked at him and squinted. "You have I.D.?"

"Uh, I left it in the car."

"One virgin Mai-Tai it is." She chuckled as she walked

away.

We ate slowly, picking at our food. I had been on edge about everything the past week, but talking to Jeff helped me feel more at ease. Our conversation drifted from how fast the summer was going, how quickly we would be heading back to school in a few weeks, and eventually to Evelyn and Neil. I also told him I had looked into Stan Caprizza a bit more on my own, but not enough to raise any suspicions. Stan was well connected in the Hershey area, and I didn't want word to get out that I was asking around about him. There had even been an article about him in the newspaper the week before. Evidently he had donated a large sum of money to the local chapter of the Boy's Club, and was honored at a recent banquet. I couldn't look at the photographs without being disgusted. Stan was playing the part of the legitimate businessman, glad-handing with the local politicians at the event, but I knew he wasn't the upstanding person he pretended to be. The fact that he was a murderer didn't help my opinion either.

"So, have you heard anything more from Detective Vaughn?" asked Jeff.

"No. I talked to him the day after we got back from New York, but not since. He's been going back over his original notes from the case to see if there was any one from the force that had taken a special interest in the investigation. It stands to reason that if Stan had someone on the inside, they might have positioned themselves to find out as much about it as they could since it involved Evelyn."

"Like getting themselves assigned as the lead investigator?" asked Jeff.

I paused.

"What are you trying to say?"

"Chad, did it ever occur to you that Charles Vaughn might have been the inside man?"

The thought had crossed my mind, and I had quickly dismissed it. But at that moment, hearing someone else say the words out loud, I was forced to accept it could very well be possible.

"I don't know Jeff, that's just crazy. If it is him, he could have easily killed Evelyn by now."

"Maybe, except now there's one more person that knows what really happened. They'd have to figure out how to deal with you before they get rid of her. Plus, for all they know, you could have told other people too. Why do you think he asked you to make the list?"

My head was spinning as I considered it. I hadn't told Charles that I confided in Jeff, and Evelyn's parents were no longer alive. So, as far as he knew, it was only myself,

Evelyn, and Neil that knew the truth. If Stan and Charles were convinced that no one else knew, they could kill both Evelyn and me, which would only leave Neil. And he had already confessed and been sentenced for her murder. If word somehow got to him that Stacy Gordon had been killed, and he claimed from prison that she was really Evelyn, no one would ever believe him.

Logically, it made sense. But I still couldn't bring myself to believe that Detective Vaughn could be involved. I hadn't known him very long, but he just wasn't the type of person to be wrapped up in something that sinister. He had also seemed genuinely affected by Evelyn's death, much like myself.

Regardless of whether Charles was involved or not, I was glad I decided not to tell Jess what was going on. As painful as it was to let her think I didn't care about her, I would have felt even worse if I put her in danger in any way. If something happened to her because of this, I'd never be able to forgive myself.

Before we realized it, several hours had passed and the restaurant was beginning to fill up with the evening dinner crowd. I could tell Mrs. Ku was anxious to make our table available for someone else, so we paid our check and walked out to the parking lot. Twenty minutes later we were back at Jeff's house. As we walked into their kitchen,

Mrs. Hall hurried in from the living room.

"Chad, dear, someone called for you while you were out. It sounded kind of important."

"Really?" I replied. "Who was it?"

"I believe it was a Mr. Vaughn or something like that. I took a message, it's here somewhere." She shuffled through the papers on the counter until she found it, then handed me her scribbled note. It said to meet him at the service parking lot at Hershey Park that night at 12:30.

"Did he say why he wanted to meet there, and why so late?" I asked.

Mrs. Hall thought for a moment, then answered "He said he had some more information about the matter you were discussing last week, but he didn't want to talk over the phone about it and didn't want you to come by his house. He also said he had to run an errand out of town today and wouldn't be getting back until late, but it was important that he showed you what he found right away."

She continued, "Is this for that journalism project you were working on? It all sounds so mysterious."

"Oh, it's nothing," I replied as I followed Jeff back up to his room.

I walked over to my usual spot in the corner and sank into the bean bag chair as Jeff flopped onto his bed.

"You're not thinking of going there to meet him, are

you?" he asked.

I really didn't want to, but helping Evelyn was too important.

"I feel like I have to," I answered.

"Do you want me to go along?"

"No, that's okay. I'm sure it's fine. Besides, I don't want anyone to know that I told you. If Charles is involved, which I don't think he is, it would just put you in danger too."

"As long as you're sure."

"I am," I replied.

Jeff nodded and returned to his copy of *Jaws*.

October 17, 1974:

Evelyn's car idled as she sat in the parking lot at Graterford Prison. She looked in the rear-view mirror and fixed her hair once more before turning off the motor. As she stepped out of the car, she could feel a chill in the air and hear the rustling of the newly fallen leaves as the wind blew them across the macadam. It was October now, and nearly five months had passed since the last time she had made the trip to see Neil. Evelyn still looked forward to their brief moments together, but over the past two years he had seemed more distant and had less to say with each visit. She hoped today would be different. The attendant looked up as she approached the front desk.

"Stacy Gordon to see Neil Fischer," she said, filling out the next line on the sign-in sheet.

"Ah, I remember you," the attendant replied. "I haven't seen you in a while."

"Yes, it's been quite some time."

"I'll let them know you're here and someone will be with you shortly."

"Thank you," answered Evelyn.

A few minutes later she was sitting in the visitation room across from Neil, separated by the wire-reinforced safety glass. They exchanged their usual greetings, and Evelyn filled him in on how her secretarial job was going and about the recent events in Harrisville. The town's Fall Harvest Celebration was the following weekend, and she would be volunteering at the Ladies Auxiliary stand handing out chicken salad sandwiches and iced tea…or coffee, if the weather didn't warm up at all by then. Neil seemed distracted, however, and she could tell there was something on his mind he wanted to say.

"What is it Neil? Please tell me what you're thinking."

"Listen, you and I both know this is pointless. I'll be in here for at least another eleven years, maybe longer if I can't keep myself out of trouble. And trust me, no one here is making it easy for me to do that. You need to get on with your life."

"What are you saying?" asked Evelyn.

"I'm saying you should walk out that door and never come back."

"You can't mean that."

"I can, and I do."

She sat still and looked at him in disbelief.

"There has to be some way to make this work. I can tell everyone the truth, and we can be together again. I don't care if it puts me in danger. I'm tired of hiding and I'm tired of not being with you."

"We both know you can't do that. And if you do, I swear you'll never see me again."

Evelyn continued to stare at him silently, her eyes starting to water.

"Ok," said Neil, "If you won't leave, I will. It's over between us. Don't bother coming here again."

And with that, he stood up and walked away without looking back. The guard opened the door on the prisoners' side of the visitation room, and Neil disappeared through the exit.

Ten minutes later, Evelyn was once again sitting in her car. A single tear ran down her cheek. So that was it, she thought. Neil didn't care about her any more, but he knew he couldn't undo what he had already done. He was trapped in every sense of the word and he probably hated her for it.

As Evelyn sat in the parking lot trying to accept the finality of his words, Neil lay on his bed staring at a worn photograph of her. He had kept it carefully hidden in his cell for years, knowing they would take it from him if they realized it was in his possession. But it wasn't hate that he was feeling. It was relief, knowing that the final sacrifice he would make for her was complete. He knew she would hurt for a while, maybe for a long time, but now she could not only live but have a life that no longer included any obligation to him. She could move on, free of any burdens. Maybe at some point she would even meet someone who could give her the kind of life she deserved.

In a moment of final resolve, his arms dropped down and extended outward over the sides of his cot. As he lay there, the photograph slipped out of his hand and fell to the floor.

CHAPTER 24

<u>Early Morning, August 13, 1978:</u>

According to the clock on my dashboard, it was 12:17 AM as I pulled into the service parking lot. I was still questioning whether I should be going alone, and several times on the drive there I had almost turned around. A gray unmarked work truck was the only vehicle in the lot. I thought to myself that Mr. Hall must have a crew working through the night on some project or another. Detective Vaughn's car was nowhere in sight.

It was a comfortable summer night and the sky was clear, so I shut off the engine and stepped out under the star-lit sky to wait. As I leaned against the car, I noticed the side gate was unlocked and hung open. It seemed strange since Mr. Hall was adamant that we keep the gate locked while working. I was too low in seniority to warrant my own key, and since I was early and there was no sign of

Charles, I decided to find the work crew and remind them about the gate.

The park had an entirely different feel late at night after closing. With the crowds gone there were only a few lights on, a lingering result of the recent energy crisis. I was pretty sure the crew would be at the Aquatheatre. Most of the other projects had been wrapped up, but there was still more work to be done there building a new stage and a storage room behind the pool. As I entered the Aquatheatre and stepped past the tiered seats, I was surprised to see it empty. A light was on in the partially completed storage room, so I walked over to see if anyone was there. It was empty.

It was then that I heard footsteps behind me on the concrete floor. As I turned around, they abruptly stopped. In the semi-darkness I could see a figure standing a few feet from the entrance. I couldn't make out who it was until he took another step towards me, and a faint beam of light from the storage room behind me illuminated his face. It was Stan Caprizza.

My heart sank as he spoke.

"Well, Mr. Anderson. It's nice to finally meet you in person. I've heard a lot about you."

I was finding it difficult to speak, but managed to get out, "From who?"

"Never mind. I'm sure you'd like to know, but it really doesn't matter. There are a few things we need to talk about."

As he came closer, I could see the glint of metal in his hand. He held a large hunting knife. I took a step backwards, trying to maintain the distance between us.

"There's nowhere to go Chad. The entrance you came in is the only way in or out, and I have it blocked. I think you'll find that all the others are locked securely."

The circular diving pool separated us, surrounded by a three-foot high concrete wall. With the old stage torn down and the new one not yet started, there was a clear path around the entire pool. I felt some relief knowing if he tried to circle around to my side, I could simply go the other way and have a pretty good chance of reaching the exit before he did. From his silhouette I could tell he hadn't exactly taken care of himself, and I knew once I made it that far I could outrun him.

"Come and get me," I prodded, feeling my confidence return.

"I know exactly what you're thinking, but I'm not that stupid. You're not going to make it out of here."

"Well, you can't get to me without making a move, so I guess we'll just stand here all night."

Stan laughed under his breath. "Ah, I see. You think

all I have is this knife."

He continued, "Of course I'd prefer to use this…it's much quieter and will draw less attention. But if you leave me no other choice, I do have other options."

He lifted his coat to reveal a .45 caliber handgun in his belt, and I felt a wave of panic wash over me. He would only wait so much longer before pulling it out and ending our standoff. I glanced around for anything to use as a weapon or for cover, but saw nothing. The only items close by were a life preserver mounted on the pool wall, and a long rescue hook near my feet. The ladder leading up to the diving platform was a few feet away, and the door to the storage room was directly behind me.

"So, what's it going to be Chad?" he pressed.

As he spoke those words, a plan formed in my mind and I knew I had to act before it was too late. I quickly dropped out of sight behind the concrete wall, grabbing the rescue hook. Before Stan could react, I reached into the storeroom with the hook and smashed the single light bulb illuminating the room. The surrounding area was plunged into darkness, giving me the opportunity I needed to grope for the nearby ladder and start the climb up to the diving platform. As much as I disliked heights, I knew it was my only choice since Stan was sure to guard the entrance to keep me from escaping. It also helped that I couldn't see how far below the floor was as I climbed.

If I could make it to the top of the platform before he realized what was going on, it would dramatically increase my chances of making it out alive. The steel dive platform would provide enough cover so he couldn't shoot me from the ground, which meant he'd have to come up after me. If he did, I'd have the advantage of both cover and a higher position above him while he climbed. If he didn't, I could just wait it out until the morning crews arrived.

As Stan's eyes adjusted to the darkness, he scanned the entire area from his location by the entrance. It didn't take him that long to realize where I had gone, but by then I was nearing the top and it was too far for him to get off an accurate shot with so little light. As I reached the top and swung my body onto the platform, I breathed a sigh of relief. I was safe for the moment.

From the ground Stan surveyed his predicament, and must have come to the same conclusion I had about his options. Before long, he began the climb up the narrow ladder.

"You're really making this difficult," he growled as he climbed, "but that just means I'm going to enjoy killing you even more."

As he neared the top I could hear his breathing getting heavier, but didn't dare look over the edge for fear of getting my head blown off. I turned my body so I was lying on my side, as low as possible, with my feet near the top of the ladder. My plan was to kick whatever stuck up first and keep kicking.

Within seconds, a hand holding the .45 appeared above the platform, the barrel pointed directly at my crotch. Before he could pull the trigger, I kicked fiercely, sending the handgun hurtling towards the ground. I could hear it rattle across the concrete floor below. Stan cursed. A few seconds later, the top of his head poked up momentarily, and I stomped at it. He ducked quickly, and as my leg extended out from the protection of the platform, I felt a searing pain rip through my lower leg. I knew instantly Stan had plunged the hunting knife into my leg, and I pulled it back with a whimper. The warm blood ran down my calf filling the inside of my pant leg, and I began to feel light-headed.

Stan saw his opportunity, and swung up onto the platform landing half beside me and half on top of me. I tried desperately to locate the knife so I could protect myself from the next attack, but then felt the blade sink into my stomach. With adrenalin now coursing through my body, I gripped the hand with the knife, forcing it away from me, and somehow managed to knee him in the groin. He groaned and pushed me towards the edge of the platform. As we struggled, my hands grasped for anything they could to keep me from falling. They found his jacket sleeve and held on, and we both rolled off the edge of the diving tower.

The fall lasted for what seemed like an eternity, and I felt myself plunge into the lukewarm water of the diving pool. As I sank towards the bottom, I had no idea where Stan was or whether he had been able to hold onto the knife as we fell. My head darted from side to side in the water as I tried to locate him in the darkness. Seeing nothing, I pushed off the bottom and propelled myself as close to the edge of the pool as I could. Blood clouded the water as I struggled to make my way to the side. Suddenly, my hand located the lip of the pool and I rolled myself out over the wall and onto the floor. A sharp pain tore through my abdomen.

As I lay on the floor clutching my stomach and trying to catch my breath, I lifted my head as best as I could to find Stan. I had no idea how bad my wounds were, but knew it mattered little if he was still coming for me. A quick glance around dispelled my fears. His lifeless body laid on the concrete a few feet away, a pool of blood growing larger beneath his head. Although I was losing blood myself and not yet out of danger, a feeling of relief swept over me as I lost consciousness.

CHAPTER 25

<u>August 14, 1978</u>:

"Has he been awake at all yet?"

"No doctor. He's stirred a few times, but he's been heavily medicated since coming out of surgery."

"How are his vitals?"

"Blood pressure is stable, and he's afebrile."

"Good. How are his wounds looking? Are they draining at all?"

"Just minimally. I changed the dressings about an hour ago. All things considered, he seems to be doing fine."

"Okay. Continue the IV fluids and let me know when he regains consciousness."

From the muffled voices and activity going on around me I could tell I was in a hospital room, but couldn't seem to move or open my eyes. As I drifted between a conscious and semi-conscious state, I tried to piece together exactly what had happened and how long I had been there. Whatever medication they had given me was too strong, however, and I fell back to sleep. When I finally woke up again, the room was dark. A monitor beeped in the background.

The flip clock by my bed read 1:00 AM. From what I could make out from the conversations I heard earlier, I guessed it had been about twenty-four hours since my encounter with Stan at the park. What I didn't know was who had found me, and how I had gotten to the hospital. Had Charles arrived there soon afterwards and found me? Was it really him who had called the Hall's residence, or was it Stan or someone else trying to lure me there?

The pain medication must have been wearing off since I was beginning to think more clearly, but my head and everything else ached. Of course, I was relieved that I no longer needed to be concerned about Stan. But the looming question on my mind was whether or not Charles was in on the whole thing and had just been using me to help locate Evelyn. The possibility was disturbing since I was entirely at his mercy, and I couldn't go to the police for fear of alerting the real inside man if it wasn't actually Charles.

Before long the night nurse came into the room to

check on me. She was middle aged, slightly plump, and according to her name tag went by Sylvia. Her eyes were kind, but she also had an air of efficiency that conveyed she had little time for nonsense. I imagined most of her patients did exactly as they were told. As I turned to speak to her the pain was almost unbearable.

"How did I get here?" I asked, grimacing. "Who brought me in?"

If it was Charles who had found me, I could be reasonably sure that he wasn't involved since he could have easily finished me off at the Aquatheatre.

"Slow down young man," said Sylvia. "You're asking a lot of questions for someone who's lucky to even be alive. You lost a lot of blood."

"But I need to know."

"Listen, I need to let the doctor know that you're awake. Once I do that, I'll try to answer all the questions I can. But only if you promise to stop moving around. I don't want you tearing any of your sutures out."

She called the front desk to have a Dr. Andrews paged, then turned back to me.

"I wasn't on duty when you came in, but from what I understand one of your friends found you and another man early Sunday morning. He called for an ambulance and the police. It's a good thing he found you when he did, or you might not have made it. The other gentleman, the one who did this to you, wasn't so lucky. He's downstairs in the morgue."

"Do you remember who the friend was?" I asked anxiously.

"I believe his name was Jeff. I heard he was a co-worker of yours and the owner's son. Evidently, he stayed here at the hospital for fifteen hours straight waiting to make sure you were okay. The other nurses finally convinced him to go home earlier this evening."

"Have the police been here?" I asked.

"Yes, they've been here since soon after you arrived. They've been anxious to talk to you."

"Where are they now?"

"Down in the cafeteria getting some coffee. I'm not in a hurry to let them know you're awake. You need the rest and I have the feeling they're going to have a lot of questions for you."

She smiled at me, then said, "The doctor will be in shortly."

After carefully checking my wounds and confirming with the nurse that my vitals were still fine, the doctor left to continue his rounds. As Sylvia began prepping a shot of Demerol for my pain, there was a knock at the door. Two police officers stood in the doorway.

"Is it okay if we come in?" asked the older one.

"Sure," answered Sylvia, "But keep it short. Mr. Anderson needs his rest."

"We'll try. Oh, and if that's pain medication, can you wait until after we talk to him? We'd like him to be as coherent as possible. It's very important."

Sylvia frowned at them and shook her head.

"You have ten minutes."

As she left the room she turned back again and repeated more loudly, "Ten minutes!"

Once we were alone, they pulled two empty chairs alongside the bed and sat down. The older of the two spoke again.

"Hi Chad. I'm Chief William Lockard, and this is Sergeant Ben Harnish."

I recognized the Sergeant's name as the friend of Charles who had provided the information that helped us track down Stacy Gordon's whereabouts.

"Nice to meet you both," I said.

"You too, son," replied Chief Lockard, "I know you need your rest, so I'll get right to it. We need to know everything you can tell us about what happened on Saturday night."

At that point I felt I'd be better off telling them as little as possible. If the corrupt cop was someone other than Charles, relating any of my suspicions to them could just alert him to what was going on. On the other hand, whoever it was could have left the police department years ago. But with no way of knowing for sure, I couldn't take that chance. So I decided to hedge my bets.

"I'm still having some trouble remembering everything."

"Just try your best," said Chief Lockard.

I proceeded to tell them how I was working with Hall Construction at Hershey Park, and had driven by late that night and noticed the service gate was open. I was going to lock it so none of my co-workers got in trouble, but decided to check if there was a work crew there first. Since there was a project going on at the Aquatheatre, I went there first. That's where I ran into Stan. I told them that he accused me of interrupting a business deal that was about to go down, and that I had better keep my mouth shut about seeing him there. I said that I assured him I had no interest in whatever it was he was doing, but I guess he didn't believe me. From there on my story followed exactly as it had happened. I knew it sounded unconvincing as I said it, and from the look on the officers' faces, I could tell they felt the same.

After they had left the room, I took stock of my situation. I was grateful that Jeff had been the one to find me, but it still left my questions about Charles unanswered. Stan obviously knew we had figured out Evelyn was still alive, and I assumed he had lured me to the Aquatheatre to find out where she was hiding. But he had never actually asked me the question, which meant there were two possible explanations. The first was that he never had the opportunity because things had escalated so quickly. The only other explanation was that he already knew which, once again, pointed towards Charles. I couldn't help but feel that time might be running out for Evelyn, and possibly for me as well. We needed help, but I had no idea where to turn.

CHAPTER 26

<u>Six Days Earlier, August 8, 1978:</u>

Evelyn tossed restlessly in her bed. She had turned in several hours earlier, but sleep hadn't come. Since Chad and the former detective left on Sunday, a million thoughts had been racing through her head. On one hand, it was encouraging to know that someone was attempting to help her and Neil after so many years. On the other hand, what did she really know about them? They seemed to be honest about their intentions, but as the years passed she had less and less faith in her ability to read people. It was a mystery to her that some people's confidence could grow as time passed, while for others, years of mistakes and disappointment could erode any capacity for self-assurance.

She was touched by Chad's attempts to bring closure

to her tragic history, and was grateful that a young man she had never known could be so committed to honoring her memory. Charles had also seemed sincere, but anyone who had been employed by the local police force at that time was immediately suspect as far as she was concerned. She knew it was entirely possible that he could have been using Chad to help track her down, and this thought had nagged at her since their visit two days earlier.

Although Evelyn had been fairly confident in recent years that her secret was safe, if the two of them had been able to figure out she was still alive and find her, perhaps someone else would too. If that someone was Stan or his partner, there would be little she or anyone else could do to protect her. Perhaps her years of peaceful existence in Harrisville had finally come to an end, and it was time to move on. But where would she go? She found herself wishing should could talk to Neil once more. Evelyn was sure he would know what to do, but she also knew that talking to him was no longer an option. Nearly four years ago he had told her in no uncertain terms to leave him alone, and she knew she would have to face this new challenge on her own.

There was no air conditioning in the home, and Evelyn usually left the second-floor windows open in the summer months to dispel the heat from the day. As she wrestled with her thoughts, she listened as the chirping of crickets and tree frogs resonated outside. It was a quiet night otherwise, and she could make out the sound of a car driving slowly up the street, stopping a few houses away. Shortly afterwards, the faint sound of a car door opening and closing could also be heard. It was much too late for her neighbor to be returning from his second shift job at Hermitage Printing, she thought. Maybe he had stopped off for a quick drink on his way home and ended up staying for several more.

She continued to listen, and for a brief moment thought she could make out the creak of the front porch steps. For several months she had considered replacing the loose boards, but had put it off for one reason or another. Evelyn had all but convinced herself she had imagined the noise when a sharp rapping on the front door broke the silence. She sat up abruptly, and the deepest fears she had tried to suppress the previous two days rushed to the surface.

A second knock followed, but she remained silent and motionless in her bed. Her first thought was to pretend she wasn't home, but with her car parked directly in front of the house, Evelyn knew that whoever stood at the front door would know she was inside. The boards creaked again, more loudly this time, as the visitor descended the steps. She quietly slipped out of bed and tiptoed over to the window to peek out. A shadowy figure crossed the lawn below her, stopping to look into each of the first floor windows.

Evelyn knew she needed to get out of the house and to her car before it was too late. Moving as quickly as possible, she slipped on the clothing she had worn earlier that day and grabbed a pair of canvas sneakers from under the bed. Unfortunately, the keys to her car were hanging on a hook in the kitchen. Evelyn debated going downstairs immediately, grabbing the keys, and leaving through the back door, but had no idea if the intruder had worked his way around to the rear of the house and was waiting there. She peered out the bedroom window a second time, trying to locate him, but saw nothing.

After weighing her options and realizing she had no other choice, Evelyn moved to the top of the stairway and descended slowly. She felt her way into the darkened kitchen, reached for the keys hanging above the counter, and took a quick glance towards the back door. Seeing no one, she took a step towards it. Suddenly, a dark silhouette appeared in the kitchen window a few feet from the door.

Evelyn bolted up the stairs as the door knob began shaking violently. Although her first instinct was to return to her own bedroom, she hesitated, then moved to the bedroom across the hallway. The room was located directly above the front porch, and its lone window opened onto the porch roof. She tried desperately to unlatch the window screen, but it wouldn't budge. At the same moment, a loud bang echoed through the house as the man threw his shoulder against the back door, trying to force it open. He tried several more times, and the next noise she heard was the sound of splintering wood as the door jamb gave way.

In desperation, Evelyn gave up on the latch and threw herself through the screen, rolling onto the porch roof below. As she slid down the roof and over the edge, her hand caught the aluminum gutter, slowing her fall. Evelyn hit the ground with a thump, momentarily knocking the wind out of her, but quickly gathered herself up. She could scarcely remember covering the fifty feet from the house to her car, but within seconds she was at the driver's side door fumbling with her keys. She prayed the intruder was still in the house and hadn't realized she had escaped through the window, but no sooner than the thought had entered her head, he was behind her. A strong hand covered her mouth, stifling her scream.

CHAPTER 27

August 11, 1978:

The past thirteen years in prison had left Neil with plenty of time to formulate an escape plan. It was inevitable given that he had the intelligence, an abundance of free time, and the proper motivation. He had carefully tracked the routines of the guards and civilian staff, knew the inner workings of the prison farm and labor programs, and had even developed a small network of support among his fellow inmates. The last part had proven to be the most challenging, since the majority of the other prisoners had little sympathy for someone who had committed the horrific crime for which he had been convicted. But there were still a handful of inmates who valued what he could do for them above anything else and were willing to overlook the unwritten rules if there was enough personal gain in it for themselves.

Even his relationship with The Dean, which had started off extremely rocky, to say the least, seemed to have settled into one of mutual respect. It was not unlike the situation with Joe Peterson years before at Hershey Park. After facing off and testing each other's mettle, they both knew where they stood and had figured out how to live together within the tenuous framework of the prison system. Their dealings had started off small, with Neil providing a steady supply of cigarettes to Dean and his gang members. Neil had decided to quit smoking when he realized a box of Camels or Lucky Strikes had far more value as a commodity than for the few moments of pleasure he would get from smoking them himself. A short time afterwards, Neil began helping Dean with various "enforcement" issues with other inmates, those that Dean didn't have access to due to differences in their scheduled free time or their location in other security units within the prison. Neil was careful, however, not to take any assignments from Dean that would jeopardize his support network.

It was through these channels he was informed that several people had called the prison to find out more about Stacy Gordon. Neil wasn't overly concerned when he learned that Chad Anderson had asked about her. Chad seemed like a decent kid, and there didn't seem to be any motive on his part other than curiosity. But when he found out Charles Vaughn had also called, he immediately began to worry. Neil had often wondered if Charles was corrupt and working with Stan, and if he ever suspected Evelyn was still alive it would only be a matter of time until he located her. Maybe he already had.

At just nineteen years old, Neil had carried out his plan to save Evelyn to the best of his ability. At the time, he knew his hands were tied and there was no way he could deal with Stan and protect Evelyn at the same time, especially without knowing who else was involved. Now, at the age of thirty-two, with Evelyn very likely in danger again, he was determined to do what he wished he could have done years before. He would find a way to get out of prison, make sure that Evelyn was safe, then go after Stan and do whatever he had to do to force the truth out of him. Once he knew for sure that Charles was involved, he would deal with him as well, either within or outside of the law.

Neil knew his escape plan had to be as simple as possible. The more complex it was and the more people he needed to rely on, the greater its chance of failure. He had formulated several different plans over the years, but had abandoned each idea for one reason or another. Neil had begun to feel the task was impossible, until six months earlier when he was assigned to the trash detail.

The garbage trucks came to Graterford three times each week at varying times: Monday at 9:00 AM, Wednesday at noon, and Friday at 8:00 in the evening. Due to the large amounts of waste generated at the prison, two trucks were needed each time. They always entered through the east entrance and stopped in a holding area until the exterior gate was closed. Both trucks were then searched to make sure no contraband or weapons were being smuggled in. When the search was completed, the interior gate of the holding area was opened and the trucks circled around an access drive to the north side of the prison where the trash service area was located. Once there, they backed into the building through a large set of overhead garage doors that were closed once the trucks were inside. It was only after those doors were closed that the inmates assigned to trash duty were permitted to enter to load the trucks. A total of four prisoners were allowed in the room at one time and were closely watched by the guard. The loading process took about an hour, and when it was complete, the prisoners were escorted out of the room before the garage doors were opened again. The trucks took the same route back to the east entrance where they were carefully searched again. The search included a thorough inspection underneath each one to be sure no one had crawled up into the undercarriage.

Neil had settled on the Friday night pickup to make his move. The plan wasn't perfect, but with time running out for Evelyn he needed to act quickly. The scheduled prisoner counts, when they were expected to be back in their cells, occurred five times each day. The last two counts were at 7:00 PM and midnight. Once the 7:00 PM count had cleared, he could leave his cell to report to trash duty and wouldn't need to return for another five hours. He also knew that the guard assigned to the Friday night pickup wasn't the sharpest tool in the shed. In addition, this particular guard had not worked at Graterford long enough to know the individual prisoners very well.

The work crew on duty that evening included Mike, Jorge, and Ethan, in addition to Neil. Mike and Jorge were both part of his network and knew their roles. Ethan was not, but could be expected to look the other way regardless of what happened.

The four worked quickly. The sooner the trash was loaded, the more time Neil would have on the outside before anyone noticed he was missing. He made sure to take a spot loading the truck on the right, which was always the trailing vehicle when leaving the prison. Mike and Jorge took their positions by the other one. Half an hour later, as they tossed the garbage bags into the truck, Neil saw the yellow-colored twist tie he had been watching for and made sure that particular bag was placed on the passenger side of his truck, near the back. It contained a set of street clothes and shoes that had been smuggled in and placed there by a friend in laundry services.

When the loading process was finished, right on cue, Mike and Jorge began shouting at each other. As the confrontation escalated, Jorge threw a convincing roundhouse swing that missed Mike's head by inches, and the guard vacated his spot by the door to break it up. At precisely that moment, another inmate similar in height and build to Neil slipped in the through the unattended door while Neil quickly dove into the back of truck, burying himself under the bags.

The guard was somewhat surprised at how easily he was able to put an end to the fight, and returned to his position at the door. He counted the inmates and, after a brief confused glance at the fourth member, seemed satisfied and waved them through doorway locking it behind them.

Seconds later, the trucks were through the garage doors and heading for the east entrance in the growing darkness. Neil had timed it on many occasions and knew it would only take about two minutes to reach the first gate, and he worked quickly to switch from his prison orange into the street clothes. After changing, he burrowed deep beneath the bags of trash. Once they were through the last gate and off the prison grounds, Neil knew they would take a left on Route 73 and pass a forested stretch of road where he could roll out of the truck before it was able to lumber up to highway speed. From there it would just be a short dash through the woods to the Township maintenance lot and salt storage area, where Neil would hot wire one of the municipal vehicles parked there overnight and be long gone before the midnight prisoner count. It couldn't have gone any better, he thought as the interior gate closed behind them at the east entrance. Neil could smell the diesel fumes as the trucks idled while the undercarriage search was completed. Only the final exterior gate remained until he would be home free. His only concern after that would be to get to Evelyn before Stan or Charles did.

But the gate never opened. Instead, the trucks cut their engines and there was silence. The only sound was the crunch of gravel underfoot as someone walked around to the back of the truck. A flashlight beam cut through the darkness, scanning the bags of trash.

"Nice try Mr. Fischer, but you can get out now," directed the guard.

Neil couldn't believe what he was hearing. Everything had seemed to be going smoothly. What could have happened? What did he miss? And as Neil crawled out from under the piles of trash, the guard gave him his answer.

"The Dean said to give you a message. He says it doesn't matter how many favors you do for him or how much you suck up to him, he's still hasn't forgotten that you tried to kill him. But he did say the two of you are even now."

CHAPTER 28

<u>August 17, 1978:</u>

Four days after being attacked by Stan, I was slowly recovering but had developed an infection from the stab wounds. As a result, I was still receiving IV antibiotics and some pain medication, which kept me drowsy. As soon as my parents found out what had happened, they booked the first flight they could get out of Frankfurt. At first my mother insisted on being with me at the hospital as much as possible, trying to sleep on two chairs pulled together in the corner of my room. I kept insisting that she needed to get more rest, and she finally relented and had spent the previous night back at their hotel.

Jeff also stopped by to see me each day after work. After initially agreeing to let me go alone to Hershey Park that night, he had begun to feel uneasy. He had waited about half an hour after I left, then decided to come check on me. He apologized profusely for not getting there sooner, and most of all for letting me go alone in the first place. I told him not to sweat it. I was also relieved to learn that the story Jeff told the authorities more or less lined up with mine. According to him, he was simply there to check on the night crew's progress for his dad, and that's when he found me and Stan. Had they bothered to look into it any further they would have found there were no night crews scheduled that evening, but at the time they seemed satisfied with his explanation.

I hadn't seen Charles in over a week and a half, and the longer it went without him contacting me, the more convinced I was he was Stan's guy. Chief Lockard and Sergeant Harnish had been back to question me again to see if I remembered anything else, or more likely, to see if I was ready to change my story. I didn't.

"Listen Chad," said William Lockard, "If there's something you're afraid to tell us, I want to assure you that we will do everything in our power to protect you. The more we've looked into Stan Caprizza, the more dirt we've been finding on him. He was involved in some pretty shady business deals, and some of his associates are not people you would want to cross."

Ben added, "If you feel you're in danger in any way at

all, you should tell us."

"No, really, I'm fine." I answered. "If I can think of anything more that might help, I'll be sure to tell you."

I could tell they were both frustrated with me.

"Well, you know where to find us if you do," said Ben as they left the room.

"And I'm glad you're okay," he added.

The more I talked to Ben Harnish the more I felt I could trust him, but I still wasn't ready to tell him my suspicions about Charles. Ben gave no indication that he knew my connection with Charles, or why Stan would have tried to kill me. As far as I knew, Charles had never mentioned my name when he asked for help tracking down Stacy Gordon. And whether Charles was involved with Stan or not, I was sure he wouldn't have mentioned to Ben why he needed the list of names or the possible connection to Evelyn Welsh. And I wasn't about to either. Evelyn's safety depended on it.

Shortly afterwards the drowsiness took over again and I drifted off to sleep. I dreamt I was in the Gold Nugget, not in a cart, but running down the dimly lit passage ways. Someone was chasing me, but I didn't know who it was or why they were after me. Fear gripped me, and a suffocating dampness permeated the building making every breath a struggle as my lungs fought for the air they needed. With every glance backwards I could see the dark silhouette of a man following me, but each time I made it around the next bend before the light could illuminate his face. As I rounded the final turn towards what should have been the exit, a brick wall blocked my path and I could go no further. I spun around in desperation, and could finally make out who was pursuing me. It was Charles. I back-pedaled as he raised his gun and took another step towards me. The cold bricks pressed against my back, their dampness intermingling with my own sweat. As he pulled the trigger, a bright flash emanated from the barrel and I awoke with a start.

I could feel the perspiration from my body soaking the bed sheets beneath me. I must have been asleep for several hours, because the room was completely black. Even the small bed-side light normally left on by the nurses was now off. I tried to remember if I had switched it off before falling asleep, but couldn't recall. Maybe Sylvia had come in and turned it off while I slept, but I was pretty sure she wouldn't have since it was usually left on.

I sat still and listened. It was dead quiet except for my own steady, rhythmic breathing. Or was it someone else breathing? It was difficult to tell in that moment immediately after waking, when the line between dreams and reality is often blurred.

But something was different, somehow out of place. I reached over to turn on the light, but as I tried the switch nothing happened. And then I realized what it was that hadn't seemed right. There was someone else in the room, standing by my bed.

"Don't move and don't say a word," said a vaguely familiar voice. I turned towards the figure next to me, but in the darkness couldn't make out who it was.

"Who are you and what are you doing here?" I asked.

My voice cracked as it formed the words.

"You did the right thing making up that story earlier."

As he spoke again I realized who it was. It was Ben Harnish.

"I'd like to know where Evelyn Welsh is. And you're going to tell me."

"I don't know what you're talking about."

"Of course you do," he said. "I know you and Charles found her. At first, I didn't know why he was asking about someone named Stacy Gordon from upstate New York, until it occurred to me that's where Neil Fischer was arrested. So, I started to put two and two together, just like you did. On a hunch, I contacted an old associate of mine. For years he was the person to go to if you needed to disappear quickly, no questions asked. As it turns out, he remembered creating a social security card and other identification for a Stacy Gordon years ago…just a few weeks before Evelyn was killed."

"But how did you know about me?"

"I didn't, at least not until I stopped by to see Charles the next day. I was hoping to find out if he was really looking for Evelyn, but he was gone for the weekend. And your car was parked at his house. I ran the plates. It turns out you made a big mistake looking into Evelyn's death."

As Ben was talking, I slowly slid my hand towards the nurse's call button hanging on the side of the bed.

"Don't even think about it," he said coolly. "You probably don't realize it, but while you were asleep I inserted a syringe of hydrofluoric acid into this IV line. If you make another move or try to call out for help, all I need to do is push the plunger."

"You're lying," I said, trying to buy some time until I could figure out what to do.

"No, I'm not."

He paused, then continued, "You know what's really interesting about hydrofluoric acid? It doesn't react with plastic, so I can carry it around in a container, put it in this syringe, and even pump it through this IV line. But when it gets into your veins, well, that's an entirely different story. First, it'll cause deep burns, killing any tissue it contacts. Shortly after that, you'll go into cardiac arrest. It's not a very pleasant way to go Chad."

I could feel droplets of sweat running down the side of my face. I knew I needed to continue stalling, at least until one of the nurses returned to the room to check on me. But I was quickly running out of ideas.

"You'd never get away with it," I told him, mustering as much confidence as I could.

"Oh, I think I would," he answered coldly. "No one saw me come back here tonight. Even if someone did, I could just tell them I found you dead when I came to check on you. No one would suspect a fifteen-year veteran of the police force."

"But if you figured everything out, why are you asking me where Evelyn is? You already know."

"No, I don't. I went to pay her a little visit this past weekend, but she's gone. Her neighbors told me she left unexpectedly and they had no idea where she was."

"That's because I moved her," said another voice in the room.

The overhead light switched on, momentarily blinding us, and Charles was standing in the doorway. His old service revolver was raised and pointing past me towards Ben.

"Drop the syringe and get down on your knees with your hands behind your head."

Ben knew it was hopeless, and with a defeated look on his face he dropped to the floor. Charles cuffed him and called Chief Lockard from the phone by the bed.

CHAPTER 29

August 18, 1978:

The following morning Charles filled me in on everything that had happened since we had last seen each other. Soon after we returned from New York, he began to feel uneasy about leaving Evelyn alone and unprotected. It may have been the intuition he had developed from years of being in law enforcement, or it may have been something else that told him it might not be safe to trust even his old friend from the police force. Regardless of what prompted it, Charles returned to Harrisville two days later to get Evelyn.

He had given her quite a scare showing up in the middle of the night, but was worried that Stan or his partner might find her first if he didn't act quickly. When his knocks at Evelyn's door went unanswered, he feared the worst and had decided to break down the door.

Fortunately, Charles had a cousin that lived in a remote area of northern Pennsylvania, and she and her husband graciously agreed to have Evelyn as a house guest until he could sort things out. With plenty of firearms and two large Bullmastiffs in the home, he knew she would be safe there.

As Ben Harnish was questioned and more details came to light, it confirmed that Charles's suspicions had been correct. When Ben figured out Evelyn was still alive and that Charles and I had located her, he and Stan needed to act quickly. Their plan was for Ben to make the trip to Harrisville the night of August 12th to take Evelyn's life. That same night, Stan would lure me to the park and finish me off there, making it look like an accident. He would then go directly to Charles Vaughn's house to tie up the final loose end. If they were successful, Stan and Ben doubted that anyone would have connected the deaths of a nineteen-year-old college student, a retired police detective, and a single woman from New York.

The plan fell apart, however, when Ben arrived in Harrisville to find Evelyn gone. Stan's death further complicated things for him, since he then had to figure out how to kill all three of us on his own before any one of us talked. If he could have been sure that no one was onto him, it would have been easy for him to just walk away from the whole thing with no one being the wiser. But he had no way of knowing how much Charles knew, or if Stan had said anything to me about him before he died. As I reflected on it, I realized that even if I had told Ben where Evelyn was, he would have killed me anyway. Once I knew he was the inside man, there's no way he could have allowed me to live. I owed my life to Charles Vaughn.

I felt guilty for suspecting that Charles may have been involved, but when I told him he just chuckled and said that a willingness to question what you know, or think you know, is a good quality for a journalist. It's pretty helpful for a detective too, he added.

With Stan dead and Ben Harnish in custody, it was no longer necessary to keep the truth about Evelyn under wraps. I watched the television from my hospital bed as the news broke that she was still alive and that Neil was innocent. The story was already all over the local channels, and was being picked up by some of the larger networks as well. A press conference was scheduled for that afternoon, and Charles was interviewed along with Chief Lockard to lay out the details of the case and how Evelyn had been found. I was a bit embarrassed, however, as both Chief Lockard and Charles Vaughn credited me with the investigative work that blew the previously closed case wide open.

Chief Lockard also announced that an investigation would be made into the automobile accident that had resulted in the death of Evelyn's parents several years earlier. In light of the recent findings regarding Stan Caprizza and his relationship to the Welsh family, the authorities were now considering it highly suspicious and felt it warranted a closer look. But it would be years before all the details of Stan's criminal activity would be uncovered, including who it was that he was ultimately working for and exactly how many people had been harmed along the way.

Within a few hours of the press conference, at least ten reporters had called the hospital wanting to talk to me. I politely declined, not only because the Chief had already related just about everything there was to tell, but also because I knew that saying anything else would have just called more attention to Evelyn and I felt she deserved her privacy. So when Sylvia came into the room telling me there was another phone call, I once again told her to make an excuse for me.

"I think this might be a call you want to take," she said.

"Isn't it another reporter?"

"Not this time. It's a young woman."

"A young woman?"

"She says her name is Jess and she's a friend of yours. She sounds cute."

I answered quickly. "I'll take it."

Sylvia had the call patched through to the phone by my bed, and I picked up the receiver nervously.

"Jess?"

"Hi Chad. How are you?"

"Better than I was a week ago," I answered with a laugh.

"I couldn't believe it when I saw the news earlier! Why didn't you tell me what was going on?"

"I really wanted to, but at first I was too embarrassed about it. I didn't want you to think I was crazy for being so obsessed with a dead girl. Then when we found out Evelyn was still alive, I knew I couldn't tell you. It could have put her in danger, and maybe even you too."

"I know. I'm sorry I wasn't more understanding. You must have felt terrible."

I assured her that it was okay, and that if I was in her position I probably would have responded the same way she had. The next hour was spent filling her in on everything that had transpired that summer with Evelyn. It was a relief talking to Jess and finally being able to lay open a part of my life that had previously been closed to her. When our conversation came to an end, we agreed to see each other as soon as we returned to F&M in a few weeks. I don't think I had ever looked forward to summer ending and school starting more than I did at that moment.

CHAPTER 30

August 22, 1978:

Several days after Ben Harnish was arrested, I was finally discharged from the hospital. Fortunately, when Stan stabbed me in the leg his knife had entered between my Achilles tendon and flexor muscle, missing both. As a result, I was able to walk with only a slight limp. My abdomen was still a little sore, but everything was healing nicely and Dr. Andrews decided to discharge me as long as I promised to take it easy and not to get into any more trouble. I told him I'd do my best, but couldn't make any promises.

Being in bed all day had been wearing on me, but there was also another reason I wanted to get out of the hospital. Neil asked that I be there with him the day he was released from prison. I hadn't seen him since my visit to Graterford over a month earlier, but he called me soon after the news came out about Evelyn. He was grateful for everything Charles and I had done and wanted to let me know. Even so, I was surprised at his request for me to be there that day. But I felt it was the least I could do for him. He had no family or friends left, and no one should have to leave prison without someone being there for them.

On a clear sun-filled Tuesday morning, I waited while they retrieved him from his cell block. As he emerged, I could see the hardened exterior he wore at our first meeting was now gone. The guard led him over to a small counter where he signed some papers and was handed the few items he had in his possession when he was arrested. They included a battered stainless-steel Hamilton watch and a black leather wallet containing a now long-expired driver's license. When he was finished, he walked over to me and extended his hand.

"Thanks again Chad. I don't know what to say other than I probably should have been nicer to you the first time we met, all things considered."

"That's alright. You had a perfectly good reason to act how you did."

Neil turned to the guard and asked, "Can I have some time alone with him before we go outside?"

"Sure," he replied, "You're a free man you know. At

least, you will be in a few minutes."

We walked over to the corner of the room and sat on a steel bench along the wall. I could tell Neil was nervous from the way he clasped his hands together as he leaned forward, studying the floor.

After a few seconds, he looked up and asked "Is anyone outside waiting?"

"Well, when I got here the press and television crews were setting up. This is a pretty big story."

"Yeah, I figured it might be. But is anyone else here?"

"Do you mean Evelyn?"

Neil nodded.

"No, I don't think so," I said. "But try not to let it bother you. I'm sure she'll want to see you at some point. But after spending years avoiding any public attention, I'm sure it would be difficult for her to be here."

"You're probably right," he replied, "I'm sure I didn't help things by telling her to stop coming to see me years ago. But it was just too difficult to see Evelyn and be reminded I would never be able to be with her. And I didn't want her to feel obligated to keep coming. I made my decision and was willing to live with it."

Neil continued, "I guess I've always just pushed people away. Even the few people I've cared about."

I didn't really know what else to say, so we sat

together in silence. I could sense that even after so many years in prison, Neil still wasn't quite ready to leave. Perhaps he was hesitant about what waited for him on the outside and if he was ready for it, and I knew that prison had left a mark on him that went beyond the physical scars he had collected during his sentence.

I gave Neil another minute, then asked, "Are you ready to get out of here?"

Neil took a deep breath, then answered, "Sure, let's go."

We stood up, and I motioned to the guard that we were ready to leave. We followed him down the long hallway to the exit. As the door swung open and the sunlight streamed in, we squinted as our eyes adjusted to the light. Neither of us were prepared for what we saw. A huge crowd had gathered, and the television crews and reporters pressed towards us to get closer to Neil. Microphones and cameras were shoved in his face from all directions as we tried to make our way to my car. Suddenly Chief Lockard and Charles were there in front of us, trying to keep everyone at bay and clear a path for us.

We pushed forward through the mob, and as the crowd finally separated a lone figure was standing in front of us. It was Evelyn. Neil saw her and froze. Her hair was the same blonde it had been thirteen years earlier, and her eyes shone a brilliant blue. Although it could have been my imagination, a trace of the innocence from years ago appeared to have returned to her face. Evelyn stood motionless for a few short seconds, then ran to him and threw her arms around his neck and kissed him. As they embraced, the crowd around them seemed to fade into the background, and for a brief moment it was just the two of them standing there. It was only then, seeing them together, that I realized the full magnitude of the sacrifice Neil had made being separated from her.

As I watched them, I thought about the past four months and all that had happened. What had caused me to become so obsessed with Evelyn's death, and what would have happened if I hadn't? I still didn't have a good answer to the first question, but the answer to the second was pretty obvious. Neil would still be in prison, and Evelyn would still be living alone in Harrisville, always wondering whether she was really safe. I also knew that things could have turned out much differently had it not been for my chance work assignment in the Gold Nugget months earlier. It had set the events of that summer in motion, which made me realize that maybe there really were no chance occurrences after all.

Looking back on it, the Gold Nugget was a pretty accurate metaphor for life. There were unexpected twists and turns, and there was fun and excitement intermingled with some frightening moments. As a rider you didn't want it to end, but when it finally did you would burst through the doors into the light, and the things you experienced were put in their proper perspective.

Until that summer, part of me felt there wasn't much a nineteen-year-old could do to make a difference in the world. But now I knew that simply wasn't true, and the best place to start was to make things right for just one person. I had started out trying to bring closure to the memory of a girl that had been dead for years, and ended up helping to give that same person a new life. I even felt a confidence that had been unfamiliar to me before, and promised myself I would never let my youth or inexperience keep me from taking a chance on something important. And that reminded me that I shouldn't wait until school started again to see Jess. Because another thing I had come to realize that summer was that she was one of those important things in life worth pursuing, and I needed to tell her. But that's a story for another time.

AUTHOR'S NOTES

The people and events of this story are fictitious, and any similarities to actual individuals or occurrences are entirely unintended. The locations, however, are real.

Franklin and Marshall College remains one of the most respected institutions in Lancaster today, with an enrollment of approximately 2,300 undergraduate students. The Fackenthal Library is still in use, though it was renamed the Shadek-Fackenthal Library after a major expansion in 1983. The motto of the college happens to be the Latin phrase *Lux et Lex,* which translated means "Light and Law". The significance of this didn't originally occur to me when I chose F&M as Chad's educational institution, but in hindsight it seems appropriate.

My intent was to be as accurate as possible with the details and history surrounding Hershey Park, but I did take a few liberties for the sake of the story. As far as I know, the Aquatheatre has never had a high dive tower, though it has hosted springboard diving demonstrations in addition to the dolphin and sea lion shows. The park was also not gated in 1965, as this story implies. Based on my research, there were no fences or gates constructed until 1971, and the park was completely open to the public with ride tickets being purchased individually. The park was also rebranded as Hersheypark in 1971 when it was transformed from a local amusement park to a regional theme park, but I chose to use the original name throughout the story for consistency.

I was also purposefully vague regarding the name of the police department that employed Charles Vaughn and Ben Harnish. While Hersheypark is currently under the jurisdiction of the Derry Township Police Department, that organization was not formed until July of 1966. According to Peter Kurie's historical account "In Chocolate We Trust", policing for the amusement park prior to that time was provided by its own security staff since Hershey was a company town.

Hersheypark continues to thrive today, and several expansions have more than doubled the size of the park since 1978. New coasters have been added over the years, and the current total stands at fourteen. The original Comet still remains, and invokes feelings of nostalgia for me to this day. It holds the distinction of being the first roller coaster I ever road as a young boy, and I can still remember my excitement as the coaster crested the first hill and descended towards Spring Creek.

The Gold Nugget, however, was the highlight of my visits there as a child. Like many others my age I enjoyed being scared, but in a way that I knew there was no real danger. In the end, the Gold Nugget fell victim to vandalism and a waning interest in dark rides. I can still remember my disappointment when I arrived at the park one summer to find it had been taken out of service. Its removal marked the end of the dark ride era for Hersheypark and, in some ways, the beginning of the end of my childhood.

JIM BOYER

ABOUT THE AUTHOR

Beneath the Lights is Jim Boyer's first novel. He currently resides in Lancaster, Pennsylvania with his wife and three children. Jim attended Messiah College where he earned a Bachelor of Science in Civil Engineering. Although his work as an engineer has taken him to various corners of the world, he always enjoys returning home to the central Pennsylvania area. In his free time he enjoys surfing, snowboarding, traveling, and spending time with his family.

CPSIA information can be obtained
at www.ICGtesting.com
Printed in the USA
LVHW110959141119
637352LV00001B/25/P